MAGIC AWAKENS

DRAGON MAGE BOOK TWO

DYAN CHICK

ILLARIA PUBLISHING LLC

This book is a work of fiction. The names, characters and events in this book are the products of the author's imagination or are used fictitiously. Any similarity to real persons living or dead is coincidental and not intended by the author.

Cover Artwork by Melody Simmons

❋ Created with Vellum

1

---

*J*immy's house really was the safest place I could be right now. It offered protection that I wouldn't get in the human world. Much of it found in the magic objects I'd brought him over the years. The vampires that worked round-the-clock security didn't hurt, either.

I'd been trapped inside the house for four days now, with the exception of my hour-long meeting with Chief Matthias. She promised me that my apartment was free of recording devices and as safe as it could be with a renegade Fae on the loose.

I still wasn't sure she fully believed me, but the video of the false me breaking into the vault had been picked apart by a team of Tech Mages and they managed to clear up the face. There was no doubt Tavas was the intruder. Every time I thought about it, rage bubbled inside me. I'd spent several hours trusting the man who had killed Jimmy. If I ever saw him again, I wouldn't hesitate to take him out.

"Morgan?"

I looked up from the couch where I was pretending to read a book to see Marco entering the room. "Any word on the dragons?"

He shook his head. "Still no sign of them in Realm's Gate. Pretty sure they're gone." Marco sat down on the couch next to me. "You doing okay, kid?"

I smiled. "As good as I can be. And, thank you for letting me stay for a few days. I'll head back to my apartment tomorrow. I'm sure you're ready to get rid of me."

"Actually, that's what I came to talk to you about," Marco said.

My forehead creased as I watched the expression change on Marco's face. He was difficult to read but I sensed his weariness, which was rare in a vampire. "What is it?"

"We had the reading of Jimmy's will today," Marco said.

I nodded. It wasn't private information, they'd had the reading in the study a few doors down from where I sat. But there was no way I was going to sit through the lawyers reading the way they were going to divvy up what was left of Jimmy.

Closing the book, I set it down. The new owner probably wanted me out of the house right away. Though, I had to admit, I always thought Marco would inherit everything and Marco would never kick me out. Being a vampire, Jimmy didn't have any remaining blood family. This organization was everything to him. And he and Marco had know each other since the Renaissance. "I can leave today, if you need me to."

"No, you don't have to leave," he said.

"That's very kind," I said.

"In fact, you don't ever have to leave if you don't want to," Marco said.

"Thank you, Marco, but I'd just be in your way, I'll head to my place tomorrow," I said.

"This is your place," he said.

I stared at him for a minute, flattered by the paternal role Marco was stepping up to fill. Jimmy had taken me under his wing when I was still a teenager, but at 23, I didn't need the kind of help I had back then. How did I explain that to Marco without hurting his feelings? To him, I must seem like a child, someone who needed protecting.

"He left it to you," Marco said.

"Wait." The words weren't making sense. "Left what?"

"Everything," he said. "Except the laundromat." Marco smiled, showing his fangs. "He left the laundromat to me."

"By everything you mean?" It was surreal. Why would he do such a thing?

"The house, his investments, his property in Sicily, the vineyards, all of it," Marco said. "You're a wealthy woman now. You never have to scavenge at estate sales again."

"Did you know about this?" I asked.

Marco nodded. "I signed as witness on the document two years ago. When you turned 21."

My heart dropped into my stomach. "Who else knew about this?"

"Nobody that I knew of." He paused. "You think that's why they killed him? For his money?"

Swallowing, I shrugged. "I still don't know why they killed him. I have to wonder about everything. You're sure nothing was missing from the vault?"

I'd asked that question every day. We'd had no sign of Tavas and still no idea as to why he would go to all that trouble to set a dragon loose on the city. Aside from finding out that I had dragon blood, there seemed to be no purpose. But if all he wanted was to know if I was part dragon, he could have skipped the theatrics and just released the dragon into Realm's Gate. It would have made more sense. There had to be something else, something bigger.

"Nothing, but when you're ready, we can do a walk through with the inventory list and you can check it for yourself," Marco said as he stood.

"Marco, you'll stay, right?" The vampire had lived in this house as long as I'd known Jimmy. It was large enough for most of his crew to crash in when needed, but Marco was a permanent resident.

"If you'll have me, I'll stay."

"Thank you," I said, still not sure what I was going to do about being the new owner of such wealth. What does one do with a vineyard and a mansion? I'd grown up with so little, needed so little, that all of this seemed excessive.

As I watched Marco leave the room, I noticed that the sun had risen in the sky. It was probably nine in the morning by now. I'd been waking before sunrise the last few days and spent most of the day on the couch.

An untouched plate of food sat nearby. Marco's attempt to get me to eat. I set the book down on the table and ran my hands through my hair. How long was I going to let myself stay locked up in here feeling sorry for myself?

My cell phone beeped, and for the first time since waking, I turned it over to look at the missed message. The whole screen was filled with text messages and alerts for missed calls. Since sending Alec and Dima home, I'd ignored all contact with the outside world. But they hadn't stopped trying to get a hold of me.

It was time to stop moping. I had to at least leave the house. Before I could lose my nerve, I texted Alec and Dima to let them know I was still alive. Then, I left the couch and walked to the guest room I'd been staying in.

The house was massive by my standards, probably by most people's standards. With eight bedrooms and ten bathrooms, countless living areas, two kitchens, a library and a study. I paused in front of Jimmy's room on my way. The doors had been closed since I arrived. What was I going to do about the house?

Was it really mine now? It didn't feel real and I wasn't sure what my next steps should be.

After considering the doorknob for a while, I entered the room. It had been empty for about a week now and it looked as it had while he was alive. I wasn't sure what I expected since I'd only been in his room once or twice when I house sat for him.

The spotted cat that called this mansion home trilled as she bumped up against my leg. It was the first time I'd seen her all week. I knelt down to pat her on the head. "Where have you been hiding?"

The cat purred and continued to nuzzle my leg. She wasn't usually this affectionate. I hugged the cat, then smoothed her fur. "I miss him, too."

When I left the room, I left the door open so the cat could roam where she pleased. It made me feel better to open it. There was something final about it. A way of finalizing that Jimmy was gone and he wasn't coming back. I wondered if that's why the door had been closed in the first place. Was that a signal to the others in the house? Either way, open or closed, there wasn't anything I could do to bring him back but I was starting to wonder if there was a way I could figure out why he had been killed.

There had to be something I was missing. So far, the police had zero leads that I knew of. James and the wild dragon were gone, and for all I knew, Tavas was gone with them. James wouldn't even know he'd been betrayed when he shifted back into human form and I had a sinking feeling that if I sat around doing nothing, I wouldn't be around by that time, either. With a sigh, I walked into my room, then into the in-suite bathroom.

The hot water from the shower beat down on my back and I breathed in the steam, washing the last few days from my hair. I thought about the vault, the dragons, what I knew about Tavas, and everything else that had happened to me. Clearly, the police couldn't be trusted. Even if there was evidence of something else missing, had that been covered up?

Marco had mentioned an inventory sheet. That was where I had to start.

Feeling energized, I finished the shower and got dressed quickly. It was time to take matters into my own hands.

2

*G*rabbing my purse, I headed down the stairs to the front door. Halfway down, I spotted a small group gathered at the entryway. Four heads turned to me and I stopped my descent while I tried to place the faces.

Marco and Scott, two of Jimmy's men were facing the door as if preventing the other two people from entering the house.

Moving slowly down the steps, I peered at the newcomers. They looked familiar, but I couldn't immediately place the sharp-nosed woman or her frizzy-haired companion.

Frizzy-hair stepped past Marco, her long black coat rustling as she walked. "Morgan?"

Marco moved to block her from me, then turned to me. "They came by to have a word with you, but I can send them away if you want."

Narrowing my eyes, I looked at the two women. Clearly not with the police, but still maintaining a sense of official business, I couldn't place why they were here. They didn't seem threatening, but then neither had Tavas. "What do you want?"

"I'm Jasmine Porter, head of the Mage Order," the frizzy-haired woman said.

"McKenzie Dowell," the sharp-nosed woman said. "I'm head of security for the Mage Order."

I tensed. The Mage Order was made up of untrustworthy, power-hungry types who would turn you over for their chance to get ahead. And that was coming from someone who worked for the mob. I'd take any of Jimmy's men over the Mage Order any day. "I've already told your Order that I want nothing to do with them."

When I was sixteen, I'd turned down an offer to attend the Order's training academy. Despite my mother working for the Order, I had no desire to follow in her footsteps. As far as I was concerned, the Order had failed her, it was their fault she was gone.

"Just five minutes," Jasmine said. "Then we'll go."

I wanted to kick them out, but there was something in her tone that made me think I should listen.

"I'll stay with you, if you want," Marco said.

"Okay, five minutes, and Marco stays," I said.

Jasmine and McKenzie both visibly relaxed. It seemed they were worried I'd turn them away. What could they possibly have to tell me that would make them this stressed out? The Order had ignored me since I left Realm's Gate and since I never joined the Mage Guild, they had no authority over me, and had no responsibility to offer me any protection.

"This way," Marco swept his arm toward the formal living room.

The women walked away and Marco hung back with me. "You sure you want to talk to them?"

"We'll give them the five minutes," I said.

He nodded. "You want them gone, just say the word."

I smiled. "Thanks." Since I'd come back, Marco had been very protective of me and I had to admit, it was sort of nice knowing that a vampire was looking out for me. There was no way I could have slept in my own apartment, enchantments or not, so he'd let me stay at Jimmy's. Knowing that the vampires that stepped in to take over never had to sleep was comforting. Someone would have to have a death wish to break into a house full of vampires.

Settling into a turquoise chair across from a gray couch, I watched as Jasmine and McKenzie sat down. Jasmine was older, probably the same age my mom would have been if she were still alive. McKenzie looked to be close to my age. Maybe even younger. It was surprising in some ways to see a younger member of the Order as Head of Security. I wondered how she'd earned that position.

"Thank you for letting us speak," Jasmine said. "I know you're not in the guild, and not involved with the Order, but we felt it was important for you to hear this."

Marco sat in the matching turquoise chair next to me and the women glanced at him before looking back at me. I was glad I'd kept him in here with me. In the past, I never would have felt scared or nervous about being alone with another Mage, no matter their title. But since Jimmy's death, my nerves have been a bit shot. It felt like my confidence was having to be re-built as I recovered from all the excitement of the last several days.

After realizing I wasn't going to speak, Jasmine continued. "There have been some kidnappings in Realm's Gate that may have an impact on you."

I looked over at Marco. "Have you heard of any kidnappings?"

He shook his head. "Been nothing on the news."

"It hasn't made the news yet, we're keeping it quiet," McKenzie said.

I looked at her. "Why?"

"We don't need to cause any mass hysteria."

"I don't understand. If there's multiple kidnappings, why

would you keep people in the dark?" I asked. "And what would it have to do with me?"

"All those who have gone missing have one thing in common," McKenzie said. "They all have a family connection to dragons."

"What the hell does this have to do with Morgan?" Marco asked. "So what if they're taking dragon bloods? That's not a surprise, really, with the history of that organization."

"He doesn't know?" McKenzie lifted her eyebrows.

Shifting in my chair, I wondered how I should respond to this. Do I deny it? Do I admit it? "There were people with dragon blood in Realm's Gate?"

"Most of the families didn't know they had dragon blood until the creatures were released a couple of days ago. Then their powers began to manifest," Jasmine said.

"Six mages have gone missing. We think they all come from dragon lineage," McKenzie said.

"I'm failing to see how this relates to Morgan. She's been cleared of the charges. The dragon wasn't her fault," Marco said.

McKenzie looked at Marco. "I really don't think it's my place to tell you."

"What's going on here, Morgan?" Marco asked. He looked hurt.

"I'm sorry I didn't tell you sooner, I just didn't know what it even meant. But I guess I'm part dragon but I didn't know before all of this happened." Without waiting to hear Marco's response, I turned back to the Order. "Wait, how the hell did you two know?"

"Your mom put it in your record when you were born. It's Mage protocol to keep a list of any known members with dragon blood," Jasmine said.

"My mom?" I leaned back in the chair, fighting against the

betrayal I was feeling. My own mother knew I was part dragon and had never told me? How was this possible?

Jasmine reached inside her jacket and pulled out an envelope. "We thought you might want to see this."

I took the envelope from her. Inside was a copy of my birth certificate, which I had never seen before. There wasn't much reason to have this document in Realm's Gate so I'd never asked my mom for it, and after she passed, it had never come up.

The date, time, and hospital I'd been born at were all recorded on the paper. Along with my mother's name and my father's name. Though he'd never been a part of my life, his name wasn't a secret. My mom told me he died when I was young, a few years after he left us. The thing I didn't expect to see was a series of empty boxes with species names next to them: siren, shifter, harpy, sprite. I scanned the list of options, until my eyes stopped on the one box that was checked: dragon.

Hands shaking, I passed the paper to Marco, who was patiently waiting in the chair next to me. He took the paper from me, then looked up. "You never knew, did you?"

I shook my head then turned back to Jasmine. "How many others?"

"You were the first who had a parent who checked that box in four generations," Jasmine said. "Your mother was part dragon. She knew her lineage and it never caused a problem for her. As a member of the Order, she followed the rules and checked the box."

"So the others, they hid it?" I asked.

"We wondered if they hid it at first," McKenzie said. "But after speaking with the families, we found out that they didn't seem to know."

"How did you find out that was the connection?" Marco asked.

"Because right before they went missing, each mage started

to manifest powers they shouldn't have been able to use," McKenzie said.

I felt suddenly sick to my stomach. "Are there any other missing mages? Anyone without dragon blood?"

Jasmine shook her head. "That's why we're here. You're in danger and we need your help."

3

$\mathcal{M}$y stomach twisted as I considered her words. The fact that I was in danger was less of the issue. The idea of helping the Mage Order was the part that was making me scream internally. After everything I'd done to gain my independence, to avoid joining the guild, to stay out of their jurisdiction, I was getting sucked back in.

Trying to seem as polite as possible, I faced the two women. "I don't know what I can do to help, and while I appreciate your concern, I think I'm pretty safe here."

"You can't stay here forever," Jasmine said.

"Sure she can," Marco said. "It's her house."

"Oh," Jasmine's eyes widened, "I didn't realize you and Jimmy were that close."

Ignoring her comment, I stood. "I think our five minutes are up. Thank you for letting me know."

"What about your duty to your fellow mage?" McKenzie asked.

Turning back to her, I crossed my arms over my chest. "Where was that duty when my mom was killed? If you and the other authorities of Realm's Gate are doing their job, why would you need me?"

I felt like an asshole for saying those words, for pretending it wasn't bothering me that others with dragon blood were missing. For all I knew, they could be my cousins.

"Look, we're not sure what's going on yet. You were the only one we have found record of in all of Realm's Gate with dragon blood, but it's clear that there were others. We aren't sure if whoever is taking those with dragon blood is finished. There could be more they are hunting down. Whatever is happening, we need to keep you safe," McKenzie said.

"I'm not going anywhere with you, if that's what you're asking," I said.

"We're not asking you to, at least not now." McKenzie looked over at Jasmine. The two women seemed to exchange a nonverbal conversation.

"Just say it," I said.

"We want you to help us find any other dragon bloods that might be out there, we need to get them hidden, protected, safe," McKenzie said.

"How would I do that?" I asked.

"We think you'd be able to detect the magic of the others," Jasmine said.

"I never knew I was part dragon. How would I know strangers were part dragon?" I asked.

"Your magic wasn't activated until the dragon came to town. We think it could be different now."

Skeptical of their true intentions, I watched them for a moment, wondering if I could read anything on their expressions. Both women were adept at keeping their faces emotionless. They probably wouldn't have risen through the ranks of the Mage Order if they couldn't hide their feelings so well. "I don't know if I want to help you on a witch hunt. What if the others want to stay hidden?"

"It's not a witch hunt, we want to protect them and without the knowledge of who they are, we don't know who the next target could be," McKenzie said.

"Then you're not very good at your job. Shouldn't you have caught this kidnapper by now?" I asked.

"We can do it faster with your help," McKenzie said. "Either way, we're going to find the perpetrator."

"So tell me, how did Tavas know that I would be able to activate the dormant dragon?" Hands on my hips, I waited for their response.

"We told you, your mother checked the box," Jasmine said.

"Which means someone broke into your records," Marco added.

I touched my finger to my nose. "Precisely, Marco. Why would I help you identify and label the hidden dragon bloods? It was your poor security that caused all of this in the first place."

McKenzie took a step toward me, fists clenched, clearly angry at my dig against her. "Hey, that was the hospital records, nothing to do with the Mage Order. Our archives have never been cracked."

"Not yet," I said. "But I watched a Fae wearing my face crack Vicious Jimmy's vault. I watched cops wipe video files that would prove my innocence. I watched hunters break into a civilian home in the human world, again wiping all computers, just to catch me and frame me for a murder I didn't commit. Why the hell would I trust you?"

"Knock-knock," a voice sounded from the front door.

I looked up to see Dima and Alec standing in the entry way, Scott standing next to them. Scott inclined his head toward Dima. "Alec vouched for this one, want me to send them away?"

"No." I glanced back at Jasmine and McKenzie. "These two were just leaving."

Jasmine handed me a business card. "If you reconsider your position, we would welcome your help."

I took the card. "Thanks, but I think I'll pass."

"Do me a favor, then," McKenzie said, holding out her own business card. "Stay here and don't do anything stupid. The last thing we need is to have to protect you."

I took her card and smiled at her in the most condescending way possible. "Good thing I can protect myself."

"Ladies, if you will." Scott took the hint that I was done talking to the mages, and swept his arm toward the front door.

Jasmine glanced back over her shoulder before she left. Scott closed the door behind them, then resumed his position in front of it as the guard.

"You okay, Morgan?" Marco asked.

"I'm fine, thanks," I said.

"Mr. Guiseppe, your two O'Clock is here," a shrill voice sounded from the foyer.

I looked over to see Kat, Jimmy's secretary. She was about ten years older than me and the only other regular employee who wasn't a vampire. With bubblegum pink hair and bright pink skin, she was a cheerful addition to the pale vampires we usually saw in this house. As a sprite, she'd live much longer than a human, or even a mage, but like me, she had no interest in eternal life.

"Thanks, Kat. I'll meet him in the office." Marco turned to me. "You sure you're okay, kid?"

"Yeah, I'm fine, go work. Pay my bills." I laughed.

He patted my cheek and left the room. The house had two entrances and business associates knew to use the back door, located near the office Jimmy had kept. Marco took over within hours of Jimmy's death in what had been a seamless transition of power. I was glad that the criminal organization I'd chosen to give my life to was civil about those sorts of things. Nothing like the Mage Order.

Kat lingered. "Sweetie, you need me to make you a sandwich or something?"

"Thanks, but I'm fine," I said.

"I could go for a refreshment, if you're offering," Alec said.

She gave him a look that could have stopped a car, then spun on her heels and walked away.

"Why are you messing with her?" I asked. "I like Kat."

"I like her, too," Alec said. "Sorry, sometimes I react before I think."

"Yeah, me too," I said. "Hey, what are you two doing here? I told you I was fine."

"You sure looked fine, being threatened by the Mage Order," Dima said. "What the hell was she doing here anyway?" Dima paused. "Did she tell you about Lyla?"

"What happened to Lyla?" I asked.

"She didn't show up for roller derby practice so I stopped by her house last night. Her dad answered the door."

My eyes widened. Lyla was not close to her parents. They lived in Winter's Haven and rarely left. The last time I recalled them coming to Realm's Gate was to see Lyla graduate from art school. If he was here, something big happened. "Her dad was here?"

"Turns out, Lyla wasn't answering his calls so he came to check on her. The cops told him they think she was kidnapped," Dima said.

"No, no, no," I said. "That doesn't make any sense, they said it was only those with dragon blood."

"You knew, didn't you?" Dima asked.

"The Mage Order said someone is kidnapping mages of

dragon ancestry. Lyla is a mage and she must have some dragon blood. That's it, right?" I asked.

Dima shook her head. "Her dad said they tested him, found some dragon blood in him."

"He wasn't supposed to tell us any of this," Alec said. "But he won't shut up about it. Says the cops are out to cover it all up. He's telling anyone who will listen."

"Shit." I turned around and pressed my palms into my temples. If the whole town knew, they'd start looking for dragon bloods. Maybe that was a good thing? Maybe people who knew and were hiding it would keep their kids safe and hidden.

Turning back around, I let out a breath. "The Mage leader told me someone is kidnapping people with dragon blood. They asked me to stay put, out of trouble and out of sight."

"But we're not going to do that, are we?" Alec asked.

"No way," I said.

"I figured you'd say that." He smiled and walked back to the front door where he'd dropped a backpack.

"What's that?" I asked.

"Snacks. We're going on a road trip, right?" Alec smiled. "There's someone we can ask for help."

4

---

*S*o far, I'd enjoyed several blissful days of peace, but I'd been in a high security home, surrounded by vampires. I wasn't willing to live the rest of my life that way.

The drive was uneventful, boring even. Thankfully, after several days of being stuck inside even the act of riding in a car down the freeway was liberating. On the drive, Alec and I caught Dima up on the first time we went to James's house.

"So, he drugged you?" She glanced at me with a skeptical look on her face.

"Yeah, but I suppose I get why he's paranoid about visitors," I said.

"You know, you could be a bit less obvious about your crush on the guy. Especially since he's friends with the Fae that tried to set you up for murder," she said.

"I do not have a crush on him!" I said, a bit too defensively.

She laughed. "Right."

"Do you have a crush on James?" Alec asked from the back seat.

"I already said I don't."

"Cause, I didn't think of it before, but Dima brings up a good point. Wasn't he the one who connected you with Tavas in the first place?" Alec asked.

"Yes, but I don't think he knew what Tavas was up to," I said, surprised at my own temper rising. For some reason, I felt the need to defend James. We might have started off on the wrong foot, but I felt like he was one of the good guys. "Besides, he shifted to save my life. You heard him when we met, he was never planning to shift. Not for anyone."

"I hear the crush now," Alec said.

Rubbing my temples in frustration, I looked up at the roof. "I do not have a crush on the guy. I hardly know him."

"I've never met the lead singer of the Chemical Zombies, but that doesn't stop me from wanting to marry him," Dima said.

I lifted an eyebrow. "Really? The dude with the mohawk?"

"Hey, you're the one who is in love with a dragon shifter who probably helped set you up for murder," Dima said. "No judgement, okay?"

Giving up, I turned back to Alec. "Do you honestly think he was in on it?"

He shrugged. "No idea. But Tavas sort of showed up right where you were, right?"

"That's true," Dima said. "And he volunteered to help pretty quickly."

"He was trying to trick us all," I said. "That's what Faeries do. Look, if James hadn't shifted, if he'd just run off on us or something, I'd believe you, but he didn't. He became the one thing he didn't want to be to keep me from being burned alive."

"Despite the fact that you seem to be immune to dragon fire," Alec added.

I opened my mouth, then closed it. There was no rebutting that comment. "Good point. I hadn't thought about that."

Both Dima and Alec stopped talking, and I sat there in silence. It was as if they realized they'd gotten to me. The last few days, I had never doubted that James was trying to help me. Him, Dima, and Alec were about the only people I had left that I trusted. Now, I wasn't so sure. There wasn't any reason for me to trust James. I didn't know him and there was no explaining the reason why Tavas has shown up in exactly the place we were at exactly the time we were there.

"Exit 291?" Dima asked.

I looked out the window. We were almost to the gas station where Chester worked. "Yes."

The turn signal clicked but it sounded so far away. What if Chester couldn't help us? What if he wouldn't help us? What if there weren't any dragon bloods out there? What if I was alone? There were too many questions spinning in my head at the moment to focus. Then, a thought hit me, and I tensed. "Do you two really think James was working with Tavas?"

"I shouldn't have said that," Alec said. "I'm sure he's a nice dragon."

"This isn't about my feelings," I said. "This is about Chester."

"Who is Chester?" Dima asked.

"The Oracle. His name is Chester," I said. "The point is, he's also friends with James. If you honestly think we need to worry about him, we shouldn't be going to see Chester."

"I think it's too late for that," Dima said.

She'd just pulled the car into a parking space in front on the convenience store and staring out front of the door with black spiky hair in tight black pants, smoking a cigarette, was Chester, the Oracle.

He tossed the cigarette to the ground and stepped on it, then walked over to the passenger window.

A lump rose in my throat as I rolled it down. "Hi, Chester."

He ducked down a bit so we were eye to eye. "You're late."

"What do you mean, late?" I asked.

He stood and took a step back. "You were supposed to be

here yesterday, but I suppose you don't care if you throw off my visions. Why would you care? You dragons always seem to think you get to control fate on your own."

Hands on his hips, he stood waiting. "You coming?"

It took every ounce of my willpower to not roll my eyes at him. Chester seemed to be a lot of work to be around. I wondered if all oracles were this high maintance. Opening the door, I stepped out. "I'm coming."

Alec and Dima joined me walking through the front door of the small gas station convenience store. As we passed by the desk, Chester waved to his aging co-worker or assistant or whatever she was. Her glasses rested on the edge of her nose as she snoozed, chin resting on her chest as she balanced on the stool at the register.

"You must not get a lot of business here," Dima said.

"It comes and goes," Chester said.

I paused in front of the door that I knew would take us to the odd cleanroom. Chester stopped walking, and turned to look at me. "Oracles are neutral, just so you know."

"I didn't say anything," I said.

"Well, you were all thinking it, and I don't blame you. But just so you know, we're not allowed to take sides. I take a side, I lose my magic. Not worth it." He walked into the broom closet that acted as the passage to his private space.

Feeling a bit better, I followed him in. Just like the first time I'd come in here, my clothes were replaced by a white jumpsuit so I matched the white floors, walls, ceiling, and furniture. The whole room still had the same eerie, bright clean quality to it that it had last time.

"What the?" Alec said from behind me.

I knew how he felt. "Don't worry," I said. "Our old clothes will return when we leave."

"I hope so," Dima said. "We look like we belong in a mental institution."

"Have a seat," Chester said. "Morgan, you going to introduce me to your friends?"

"Don't you just know who we are?" Alec asked.

Chester glanced at me. "I can see why you hang out with him, he's just like you."

"Alec, Dima, this is Chester. He's an Oracle, but not a mind reader," I said.

"That's nice," Alec said. "No tea, right?"

"No, I don't play by the rules your dragon friend does," Chester said.

"I thought he was your friend," I said.

"He is my friend. But as I already said, I can't take sides. That's why you never get a straight answer from an Oracle. Why we can't tell you exactly what to do or exactly what the outcome will be. Oracles have to give all fates a chance."

"All fates?" Dima asked.

"There's never just one version of the future," Chester said. "Right now, I see four options."

"For what, exactly?" I asked.

"Your life," Chester said. "Or your death."

Goosebumps rose on my skin and I shivered. "I didn't come here to ask about that."

"What do you mean her death?" Alec asked.

"I'm just saying, the quest you've chosen to follow will have consequences. All actions have a result. The choices you make, and the choices others make, will determine the outcome."

"Right, that's helpful," Alec said.

"Don't worry about it, Alec. He won't give a straight answer to the future no matter what he gives us," I said.

"That hurts. After everything I told you last time, I thought you'd be a bigger fan," Chester said.

"You didn't give me anything that would help, just a reflection on how things played out," I said.

"Didn't I?" he said.

"You just said that help would come from the place I'd least expect," I said.

"And how did you solve your problem?" he asked.

"Me," Dima said.

Chester smiled.

"There was no way I could have known that going in," I said.

"But you could have been more weary of that Fae you were trusting because you trusted James," Dima said.

"That's true," Alec said.

"Alright, I get it. Morgan fucked up," I said. "Can we stop focusing on the past and figure out what we came here for?"

"What did you come here for today?" Chester asked.

"We're trying to find the missing mages. The ones with dragon blood. Do you know where we could find them?" I asked.

"You've already met the surviving Dragon-Bloods," Chester said.

"When?" I asked. "Are they hiding in Realm's Gate?" It shouldn't come as a surprise to discover that the secret organization was hiding in plain sight in the magical community I called home.

"No," Chester said.

"Where?" I asked.

"Soon," Chester said. "But first, a prophecy."

5

I leaned back against the cushion of the sofa. Why couldn't things just come with answers? Why did I have to go through all this to get to the point? "Let's hear it."

"It's not for you," he said, turning to Alec, "It's for your vamp boyfriend."

"Oh, he's so not her boyfriend," Dima said.

"And you're involved, too," Chester said, smiling at Dima.

"Me and the vamp?" Dima asked.

Chester nodded. "When twice by time your fates are tested, you'll rise to find the help you need."

"What the hell does that mean?" Dima asked.

"You'll know when it's time," he said.

"You're not going to help us, are you?" I asked.

He smiled. "You know me better than that by now, don't you, love?"

I wasn't sure if I knew the Oracle at all. Inside the gas station, he seemed like another college dropout who wished he was a magician. Here, he was like the caterpillar from Alice in Wonderland. Or maybe worse, the Cheshire Cat. "I honestly wouldn't be surprised by anything at this point."

"Can't you just give us any tip on how we can find our friend?" I asked.

"Honestly, I'm rather surprised you're not here asking about James, seeing as how you two will eventually be an item and all that," he said.

"I totally called it," Dima said. "And I never even met the guy."

"You know, we're not that far off on the family tree," Chester said to Dima. "Most Sirens have at least a hint of the second site."

Turning to me, Chester pointed at Dima. "If you're smart, you'll listen to this one."

Face hot, I took a deep breath. "James and I are just friends. And he's off being a dragon right now. He won't even be back to human form for a while, so no, I'm not asking about him."

"Oh, he's already back in human form," Chester said. "And they've got him locked up, too."

My chest tightened. "Who has him?"

"The Dragon-Bloods." Chester said it as if I should have known all along.

I took a deep breath. "Wait, the same people who have the missing mages?"

He shrugged. "Who knows, those Dragon-Bloods have been unstable for years."

Narrowing my eyes at him, I searched his expression. "You're not telling me something. You know, you could help me."

"That's the thing, Morgan," Chester said. "This time, I don't want to help you. There's four possible outcomes, like I said. Two don't end well for you and in both of those, I help you."

Lowering my head into my hands, I took a few breaths. This was not what I was expecting. We'd wasted half a day making this drive, and we were no closer to finding Lyla. On top of that, I now knew that James was in danger. Looking back up at Chester,

I stood. "Is there anything you can tell me? Are my friends safe? Will I be able to help them?"

"For now, but you've got less than 48 hours to find them both," Chester said.

"What's going to happen in 48 hours?" Alec asked.

"Ritual sacrifice, you know, the usual," Chester said.

"Usual?" I said. "In what world?"

"When you've lived as long as I have, you see a lot of things," Chester said.

"What can you tell me?" I asked.

"The Mage Order," Dima said.

I turned to her. "What about them?"

"They said they wanted your help, right? They're looking for the same missing mages as you," she said.

"Told you, you need to listen to this one," Chester said.

"You want me to go to the Mage Order? The people who let my mom die and tried to cover it up?" I asked.

"There are things you don't know," Chester said. "They can help."

"You know, it might not be a bad idea," Alec said. "It's not like we have to join them, just find out what they know."

"That's not how mages work," I said. "We get their help, we'll owe them."

"Chester, will they know about James? Is it the same people?" I asked. My intention in coming here had been all about finding the missing mages, but now that I knew James was in danger, there was a part of me that wanted to help him first. After all, he did save my life, no matter what Dima and Alec said. And despite my attempts to suppress my attraction to him, I'm sure that played into it at least a little.

"I'm not sure," he said. "From what I've seen, both are in the hands of members of the Dragon-Bloods, but I can't tell if they're connected. Their order has been in chaos for the last few centuries."

"We don't have a choice," Dima said. "We're going to need the help of the Mage Order."

"We'll find him, Morgan," Alec said. "I'm with you until we do."

"Me too," Dima said. "I've never met a dragon, might be a wild ride."

I glared at her.

"Not like that," she said.

"Alright. I guess I don't have a choice." I looked at Chester. "Anything else you can tell us?"

He shook his head. "Sorry, but James would kill me if I did something that might hurt you."

"Wait," Alec said. "You've seen the two of them together, right?"

"Not the time for jealously," Dima said, hands on her hips.

"No, it's not that," Alec said. "You've seen a future where James is safe, and Morgan is safe."

Chester nodded. "I have. But as I've said, there are multiple versions of the future."

"But you seem so intent on that version," Alec said.

"It's my favorite." Chester shrugged. "Been a long time since James has been happy. Besides, it's the most likely version if you all survive the next 48 hours."

"That's it?" Alec said. "No other clues?"

Chester tapped his chin with his index finger, lips pursed in thought. After a moment, he pointed at me. "Tavas."

Tension rose inside me and I prickled at the name of the Fae who had betrayed me. "What about him?"

"You'll have to get over whatever he did to you," Chester said.

"Nope, not happening," I said.

"Tavas is important," Chester said. "You'll need him."

"You can't trust him," I said. "You can't trust any of the Fae."

"Well, that might be true, but it doesn't mean you can't work toward a mutually beneficial end. That's the key with someone like Tavas. He's only on his side. He won't do something to help another unless it benefits him."

"You can't be serious?" Dima said. "Tavas double-crossed her."

"You asked for my help," Chester said. "This is me helping you. Go to the Mages. Find a way to work *with* Tavas. You do those things, you might make it out of this alive."

"Our meetings are always so cheerful, Chester," I said.

"Curse of being an Oracle, I suppose. There's more bad news to deliver than good. People never seem to come to me when things are good," he said.

I hadn't thought of that. I probably wouldn't feel any need to consult him if I was happily living my life in Realm's Gate. A vision of me and James curled up on the couch together briefly filled my mind. Clearing my throat, I pushed the thought away. There was no way to know if that was in my future. At this moment, I didn't even know if any of us would survive the next 48 hours. If we made it through this, we'd have reason to celebrate. "Tell you what, Chester. When this is over, I'll come back. You can give me some good news for a change."

"Sounds perfect," he said. "Now, clock's ticking. You need to go."

"What happens when the clock stops, exactly?" Alec said. "When you said ritual sacrifice, you didn't actually mean..."

Chester made a slicing motion with his finger across his throat. "It's just like it sounds."

Dima's keys jingled in her hands. "Let's stop wasting time."

We turned toward the door that led us out of the clean room. I paused at the doorway while my friends moved on ahead. Turning back, I saw Chester sitting on the couch.

Taking a few steps into the room, I moved closer to him. "There's something you didn't say, isn't there?"

He looked up at me, all mischief gone from his face. "Tavas didn't kill Jimmy."

At first, I thought I'd misheard him. "How is that possible? I saw the video."

"You're going to have to trust me on this, okay?" Chester said.

I nodded. "It still doesn't mean I like him."

Chester smiled. "Go."

6

Running to the car, I threw myself in and slammed the door. "Gun it, Dima."

She started the car and we headed toward the on-ramp for the highway. "You went back."

"I did." I glanced over at the speedometer. She was already going fifteen over and I watched as the needle moved up, pushing closer to 90 miles an hour. It was like she knew.

"How bad is it?" she asked.

"Not bad, necessarily," I said.

"What is it?" Alec said from the back seat.

"Chester said that Tavas didn't kill Jimmy," I said.

"That's a good thing, right?" Alec said.

"It is," I said, feeling empty. "But now that means we have no idea who the real killer is." I couldn't explain it, but I felt like I was back at ground zero.

"We'll worry about that later," Dima said. "I know how important this is to you, but when this is done, I'm in for another crazy adventure to help you find the real murderer."

"Besides, maybe Tavas will know who did it," Alec said. "We just need to ask the Mage Order to help us find him."

"It's not that easy," I said. "The Mage Order isn't going to want to help us find a dragon. They only care about their own kind. The only reason they're even helping the missing people is because they are all mages."

"Well, we'll tell them we won't help unless they help us find James," Alec said.

"They'll want payment up front," I said.

"Can't you borrow the money from Marco?" Alec asked. "I'm sure he'd give it to you."

"That's not the kind of payment they'll want," Dima said.

"They asked for my help already. So I know what they want. They want me to find any other mages with dragon blood who live in Realm's Gate," I said.

"How would you do that?" Alec asked.

"I have no idea," I said. "The best we can hope for is that once we tell them we saw an oracle who told us the stakes, they'll let us skip that part and just go look for the missing mages. We could get lucky and find James while we're looking."

"There has to be something better we can do to find him than hoping for good luck," Alec said.

"Chester told us to go to the Mage Order. It's our best chance," I said.

"You're just going to give up on him?" Alec said.

"What the hell am I supposed to do? You have any ideas, Alec?"

The car was silent. I could feel the tension hanging between us all. We wanted to save Lyla and I knew my friends wanted to help me save James. But sometimes there were things you couldn't control. "Let's just get to the Mage Order. We'll figure it out from there."

There wasn't much conversation on the drive back to Realm's Gate. My stomach felt like a lead weight as I wondered what Lyla and other mages were doing right now. And while I tried to focus on them, the people from my home town, my old childhood friend, my thoughts would wander back to James. He was thousands of years old. Surely Chester was wrong. How could he be trapped by the Dragon-Bloods?

I remembered when we first met. He'd seemed so paranoid and worried that he thought I might be a threat. He said he could sense my dragon blood. He was really afraid of them. What did the Dragon-Bloods have that made them so terrifying?

"Dima," I broke the silence, "do you remember learning about the Dragon-Bloods in school?"

"A little," she said. "But it was always one of those things, right? Where we didn't know the full story. I just assumed they were either all gone, or maybe that they never even existed in the first place."

"That's sort of what I thought, too," I said.

"What did you learn about them?" Alec asked.

"Like she said, it wasn't much." I thought back to high school, trying to recall history class. "Mostly, we were just told they were bad. I can't recall the details as to why."

"That's because you were too busy staring at that new kid that joined our class late. What was his name?" Dima asked.

I laughed, remembering the dark haired new student that all the girls were swooning over for months. "I can't remember. Wow, I guess that makes me a terrible person. There were only like 50 kids in our class."

She shrugged. "I don't even remember the name of the guy I lost my virginity to, so I think you're okay."

"Alright, new subject," Alec said.

Dima and I were laughing in the front of the car, tears streaming down my face. It had been a long time since I laughed so hard. And it wasn't even that funny. "Feels good to laugh."

"Promise me something," Dima said. "When this is over, we do something fun together. Nothing that involves saving the world. I missed you."

"I missed you, too," I said. We'd been friends in high school and the issues that drove us apart seemed so trivial now. "And I think that's a great idea."

"Hey, what about the new guy?" Alec asked.

"You can come along, too," Dima said.

The next few hours passed by with Dima and me telling Alec stories about growing up in Realm's Gate. He was fascinated by even the most mundane events and situations. I understood, though. After living in the human world for a few years, I could see how different our lives were.

The jovial mood subsided as Dima slowed the car to turn onto the winding road that would take us all home. Silence once again filled the car.

None of us spoke until the car was through the barrier, in Realm's Gate, headed to the Mage Order.

"So we just drive up to the Mage Order?" Alec asked.

"I guess so," I said. "They already asked for my help, so they shouldn't have a problem with me showing up."

"What about us? I don't see a whole lot of Mages who are okay with Vampires," Alec said. "Or Sirens."

"They'll have to go with it if they want help. Besides, you two have been there every step of the way. They should be begging for all of us to help," I said.

Dima turned onto the tree-lined street where the brick mansion that housed the Mage Order stood on a street that used to only be allowed for Mages to live on. Technically, no such restrictions could be in place any longer, but I doubted there was a single family that lived on the wealthy street that wasn't of Mage descent.

"That's it, right?" Dima pointed to the gated house in front of us.

"Damn, I thought Jimmy's place was impressive," Alec said.

Dima turned on the ridiculously long driveway and stopped at the security booth in front of the gate. I leaned over so I could see through Dima's now open window. The security guard left the booth and walked over to the car, leaning down to look through the window.

"Good evening, ladies," the security guard said with a smile. He wore a pressed navy uniform with gold buttons and a matching hat. He was well put together and smiled with straight white teeth. But I knew appearances could be deceiving when it came to Mages. I could feel his magic pulsing off of him. It hit me like the bass lines at a rock concert. This guy wasn't just a low-pay security guard. The Mages had pulled out all the stops.

"What can I do for you this evening?" he asked.

"Hi," I squinted to see the name on the shiny badge on his chest, "Matt. My name is Morgan Drake. I believe they'll be expecting me."

"You, yes, company, not so much," he said, not breaking his smile.

"They've been to the Oracle with me. I need them," I said.

That caused the smile to fade. "One minute." He ducked back into his booth and picked up a phone.

We waited.

"Maybe we should just go," Alec said. "Try to find a way to do it on our own."

"Chester said we needed to come here," Dima said. "We have to give it a shot."

A rumbling sound, followed by a squealing noise, filled the air. I turned toward the sound and noticed the gate was swinging open.

"Go on in," Matt yelled from the security booth.

I smiled and waved, then elbowed Dima. She got the hint and smiled and nodded at Matt as we slowly drove in to the compound.

The driveway was a half mile long, lined with tall trees that, thanks to the magic enchantments on them, stayed in an eternal autumn. Red and gold leaves that never fell. Lit by floodlights and sparkling LEDs that were supposed to be festive, it had an otherworldly feel to it.

"It's beautiful," Alec said.

"Right, or artificial and a completely unnecessary use of magic and resources," I said.

"Why do you hate the Order so much?" Alec asked. "I mean, I know it has something to do with your mom, and I know they're a bunch of elitist assholes, but it seems bigger than that."

"If we survive this," I said. "I'll tell you all about it."

"Yeah, I'm starting to wonder if we should have turned around when he suggested it," Dima said.

I turned away from Alec, back to the front of the car. Outside the windshield, I saw the front of the building and goosebumps rose on my arms. There were at least a dozen people standing outside the door. What were they all doing there?

"Should I gun it?" Dima asked.

"No," I said. "We're already in. We try to leave, they'll just use magic to trap us."

"Well, been nice knowing you," Dima said.

"We don't know that they'll hurt us," Alec said. "Maybe they're here to help."

Either way, I wasn't thrilled with the idea of so many Mages being in the same place at the same time. I hadn't been around more than a couple of mages at once since leaving the community I'd been raised in. And usually that was by chance at the grocery store or the Dizzy Dragon.

Dima stopped the car in front of the doors to the building.

Tan and brown brick with latticed windows covered the massive three story structure. I looked on it as if it were my prison rather than a place of welcome. I hoped it wouldn't turn out that way. "Well, what are we waiting for?"

I opened the door and stepped out of the car.

7

*T*he Mages stood at attention, their eyes following us as we gathered near the passenger door of the car. My chest felt tight as I waited for them to make the first move.

Finally, movement out the corner of my eye alerted me to Jasmine, the head of the Order. She wore a long dark skirt and a floral blouse with loose sleeves that fluttered as she walked. Bangles on her wrists jingled as she moved.

Behind her, McKenzie, the head of security followed. Today she was wearing jeans and a Chemical Zombies tee-shirt, still not looking the part I'd expect for a person holding her title. Maybe that was part of her strategy.

"Morgan," Jasmine clasped her hands and nodded in the traditional Mage greeting. It had been years since anyone had used the formal gesture on me. She didn't even use it when she came to see me this morning.

Tangled between my upbringing and a sense of rebellion, I half reciprocated, nodding, but not adding the hand gesture. "Jasmine, McKenzie." Looking behind me, I swept my hand toward each of my friends. "This is Dima, and this is Alec. They're helping me find the missing Mages."

McKenzie's eyebrows rose in surprise, but she kept quiet, seemingly waiting to see how the older mage responded before she spoke.

Jasmine, to my surprise, clasped her hands and nodded to each of my friends. "Welcome, you are true friends to help with such matters."

Working to keep the suspicion from my face, I stared at Jasmine and McKenzie. Had the Order changed since I'd last dealt with them? Since my mother's funeral, I'd avoided them at all cost.

Doing my best to be civil, I smiled. "That they are."

"We are so happy you've decided to help us on our mission to save the other dragon mages," Jasmine said.

"Yeah, we're going to have to talk about that," I said. "We have some things that need taken care of first."

"Oh?" Jasmine swept her arm toward the double doors at the front of the house. "Why don't you come in. We can discuss what you need to take care of."

My breathing grew shallow as I followed her across the threshold. There were so many memories in this building. Meeting my mom for formal functions, attending ceremonies when she moved up in rank, holiday parties.

I stopped, frozen, and stared at the formal parlor to the left of the main entryway. The rest of the group moved ahead of me, but I couldn't move. The scene from that day played out in my mind. I could still picture the chairs and people dressed in black. The little paper plates filled with various food items they wanted me to eat. Conversations happening all around me despite the fact that we were gathered to remember my mother. The rest of the world had moved on, and mine had ended.

The mages said they'd be there for me, but just days after her funeral, charges were brought against my mom, saying she'd neglected her duty. How quickly they'd turned on me. When the charges were dropped in a matter of days, after the hunters finally caught her partner, the one who was really to blame, they tried to apologize, but the damage was done. It had been another mage that betrayed my mom. And the very mages who said they'd be there for me had turned their backs on me when they thought I was the daughter of a traitor. I left the next day.

"Morgan?" Alec's hand was on my shoulder.

Shaking myself from the vision, I looked up at him. "Sorry."

"You okay?" he asked.

I took a deep breath. "Yeah, just been a long day."

We turned and caught up to Jasmine and Dima, who had stopped at a formal sitting room. I looked behind me and realized we were alone. "Where are the others?"

It was hard not to be suspicious of the mages. There were a dozen of them outside, and now we were alone. Were they preventing us from leaving? Had we made a mistake in coming here?

"Those are our perimeter guards," Jasmine said. "Since the dragon incident, we've learned there are more dragon mages than we thought. Several of them came to us. We're hiding them in this building so they remain safe."

"Hiding them?" I stiffened. "Like in the basement or something?"

"Of course not," Jasmine sat down, "they have guest rooms. There are no prisoners here."

I bit down on the inside of my cheek to prevent myself from saying something I might regret. It was proving more of a challenge than I thought it would be to come back here.

"Please sit," Jasmine said.

"It's okay," Alec said. "We're not going anywhere."

With a nod at him, I sat down on the couch facing Jasmine's chair. Alec sat next to me and Dima took the chair next to Jasmine.

"So, how did the three of you come to be involved in all of this?" she asked.

"Not everyone is afraid to mingle with those who are different," I said.

"Morgan," Jasmine leaned forward in her chair, elbows resting on her knees. "I know what you've been through. I was there. I witnessed the way you were treated and it wasn't right. If I had been the one in charge, that never would have happened."

"Serendipity," Dima said.

"I'm sorry?" Jasmine asked.

I turned to Dima, curious where she was going, and thankful that she spoke up.

"There were a series of serendipitous events that connected the three of us, and now we're all a part of it," she said.

Jasmine leaned back. "I see. And the break-in to the daylight cells? That was to rescue you?" She nodded at Alec.

"Yes," I said. "It's been a busy week."

"I would say so," Jasmine said. "Morgan, I wish you would have come to us right away. We could have helped you from the beginning."

Eyebrows raised, I stared at her.

"Fair enough," Jasmine said, answering my silent protest. "But at least let us try to make it up to you."

"Okay," I said. "I need help finding a Fae named Tavas."

Jasmine flinched. "Isn't that the wanted Fae that all the police are searching for? The one who killed Jimmy?"

"Possibly," I said.

"This isn't the time for a vendetta," Jasmine said, "I know you're hurting..."

"It's not about that," I said.

"It's the Oracle," Alec said.

The room grew silent and we all stared at Alec.

"You've been to an Oracle?" Jasmine said. "Recently?"

"A few hours ago," Alec said. "He said we have to find Tavas to put a stop to all this."

"If we find him, we'll be able to save the missing mages," I added.

Jasmine sat quietly for a moment, as if she was contemplating how to turn us down or re-direct us in a direction she wanted. Internally, I prepared to threaten to leave.

"Alright," Jasmine said. "We'll help you."

"You will?" I asked.

"I do expect your help in return," she said.

This wasn't unexpected. The whole magical community ran on favors. I just hoped that I'd be able to find out what was expected of me before I agreed this time. James still had a favor to play. A little rush of panic fluttered inside me as I wondered if he'd survive long enough to cash it in. "Of course. What would you need me to do?"

"The mages with dragon blood," she said, "especially the younger ones, will need some guidance and support. Things are going to change for all of you now that you've been exposed to the magic of the dragon. If you haven't felt the changes yet, you soon will."

I nodded, thinking back to making fire without words. Quickly, I focused on other things, not wanting to spontaneously combust in here. James had said something similar, that I'd need to learn to control it. "I've noticed, but I'm not sure what you want from me. There's nothing I can do to help them."

"But you can," she said. "There are a lot of younger Mages that look up to you."

"Why?" The word came out harsher than I meant.

"Because you left, you made it on your own. Things are changing, old traditions are dying. More mages than ever are choosing to live in the world outside of Realm's Gate."

"Wait, are you saying the kidnapped mages were living in the human world?" Alec cut in.

Jasmine turned away from me, to look at Alec. "All the missing mages were either living in or visiting the human world when they were abducted."

That made things more complicated. If they were taking mages from the human world, did that mean they were hidden there? The human world was huge. They could be anywhere.

"Even if I agree to help, I don't think there's anything I can do. I don't know anything about being a dragon mage," I said. "I didn't even know that was possible until a few days ago."

"This might help," a new voice said from behind me.

I turned to see McKenzie holding a book. She extended her arm, offering it to me.

After taking the book, I stared at the brown, leather cover. "What's this?"

"We think your mom left it for you," McKenzie said.

"What do you mean *you think* she left it for me?" I asked.

"It appeared a few hours after the dragon attack, at the seat your mom used for Order meetings." McKenzie pointed to the book. "Look."

I looked down at the book and noticed that there was an embossed name on the cover: April Drake. I could feel the blood draining from my face as I stared down at my mother's name. "It just appeared? How is that possible?"

"I think it was dragon magic," Jasmine said. "She must have known a spell to make it reappear if a dragon came by."

Only half hearing her response, I opened the book. It smelled like old parchment, and roses, just like my mom. On the first page was a letter, addressed to me.

Dearest Morgan,

If you're reading this, I'm gone and things are changing around you. Nobody should have to carry the burden of our bloodline alone. It's possible you'll never encounter a dragon, and never need this book, but if you do, and you're reading it, there is much you must learn. I've filled these pages with all I know. I wish I could be there to help you myself, but I know you can do this. You are a brave young woman. I love you. Mom

Tears blurred my vision and I wasn't sure if I was angry that my mom never told me, or happy to have something of hers after all these years. Whatever I was feeling, it had to wait. Wiping my eyes, I swallowed back the lump in my throat. Sniffing, I closed the book. "It doesn't explain why I'd be any good at doing this."

"You've got help in that book," McKenzie said. "We don't know anything about Dragon magic, or what it will do when mixed with a Mage. We don't know if it even reacts the same to all of you. But you've got some authority with that book and we think the others will respond to you."

"It makes some sense to me," Alec said. "And it's not a bad deal."

I glared at him. "You think it would be a good idea for me to be teaching others how to do something I don't even know how to do?"

"You have James," Dima said. "If we find him, I bet he'll help."

"Who's James?" Jasmine asked.

"Nobody," I said. "A friend. He's missing, too."

"Another missing mage?" McKenzie said. "That's up to seven, then."

Jasmine's expression darkened and she looked up at the other woman. "You sure?"

McKenzie nodded. "Seven if their friend is missing, too. At least that we know of."

"Why does that matter?" Dima asked.

"Mage thing," I said. "Seven is a powerful number. It's purposeful. Nothing is a coincidence when it comes to magic."

"But James isn't a mage," Alec said.

"Doesn't matter," I said. "Seven with dragon blood, it has to mean something significant."

"What if they're just getting started?" Dima asked. "What if they take more? Maybe it doesn't mean anything."

"If they wanted all those with dragon blood that they could find, they wouldn't have framed me and risked my life. They would have just taken me first," I said. "This is purposeful."

"I agree," Jasmine said. "It's dangerous for all of us."

I stood. "We have to find Tavas. We need a locating spell. You in?"

Jasmine rose from her seat in a graceful swirl of fabric. "Divination room. Five minutes. I'll find the other eleven."

"Other eleven?" Alec asked as Jasmine and McKenzie hurried away.

"We need thirteen for a locating spell. I told you, numbers are a big deal," I said, taking a few steps in the direction of the divination room. Pausing, I turned to my friends. "You two have to wait here. You can't follow me into that room."

"Why not?" Dima asked.

"Yeah, we'll be fine," Alec said.

"No, you won't. It's too much magic in one place at one time. It's dangerous to anyone without Mage blood." I handed the book to Dima. "Guard this with your life."

8

*T*he divination room looked just as I remembered it. While I'd never actually performed any spells in this room, I'd wandered through all the rooms on this floor while waiting for my mom often as a child. Now, I found myself being asked to take a seat.

I ran my fingertips over the smooth, polished wood of the table. It had exactly thirteen high-backed chairs with embroidered cushions on the seats and backs. The black marble floor sparkled in the light of the crystal chandeliers. My mom told me the marble was imported from the Fae Realm long ago, before it was closed off.

Facing the door, I leaned against the back wall, wondering how long the spell would take. We'd been given a time line and I wasn't sure how long it would take to find Tavas. And until we found him, we couldn't go after the dragon mages.

McKenzie walked into the room, alone. "You sure about this?"

"About what? The spell?" Before I even finished speaking, I realized what she meant. "You mean Tavas, right?"

She nodded, then leaned against the doorframe. Arms

crossed, her posture radiated unwelcome and resentment. It was obvious that she did not agree with Jasmine on this venture.

"Look, I have every reason to hate the guy. But the Oracle says he didn't kill Jimmy and that he's the key to figuring all this shit out. So unless you have a better idea, I need to find him. Fast."

"You never told us about the rest of your visit with the Oracle. What else did he say?" She dropped her arms and walked over to the table and rested her arms on the top of one of the high-backed chairs.

"I told you the important stuff," I said.

"I doubt that," McKenzie said. "You see, I have a gift that very few mages have. It's one of the reasons I do what I do."

The hair on the back of my neck stood on end as I kept my eyes locked on hers. What was she talking about? And where was everyone else? "And what gift is that?"

She moved away from the chair and walked around the table, stopping next to me.

It took a lot of willpower to keep from stepping away from her. She wasn't a large woman. She was a few inches shorter than me with a petite build. But she sure was good at striking an intimidating pose.

"Are you threatening me?" I asked.

"No, but you might want to start telling the truth. You want to know my gift?" she asked.

Not willing to indulge her, I remained silent. Waiting for her to respond.

She smirked. "I know when people are lying. And you are not telling me the truth."

I laughed, tossing my head back. She had nothing on me. Even if she had the ability to sense when someone was telling the truth, she couldn't dig around in my head. Only those with psychic gifts had that ability. And mages could never gain that level of mind-reading. She was probably part oracle, or part siren, getting some of their magic, but wasn't powerful enough to use it for much.

"What's so funny?" McKenzie's brow furrowed. She took a step back.

I probably looked like a crazy person, which was fine. "You think you're tough. But I've seen your type before. Raised in the human world, finds out about Realm's Gate, someone tells her she's special, she feels important. And now, that girl is hungry to prove herself. Did I miss anything?"

McKenzie glared at me.

I'd probably been a bit too harsh, people who weren't natives to Realm's Gate didn't like when others found out. I wondered what her retaliation would be, then realized it didn't matter. The Mages wanted my help, which meant, on some level she had to at least be civil.

Before she could speak, Jasmine walked into the room, followed by almost a dozen people I didn't recognize. The group filed into the room, the only sounds were their shoes against the stone floor.

I looked over at the still silent McKenzie, her mouth turned down in a scowl. She seemed like she wasn't letting go of what I said to her.

Jasmine walked over to her and rested a hand on her shoulder. "McKenzie, we'll see you after the ritual."

Forcing myself to hold back a gloating smile, I watched the other mage go. While her gift for knowing when someone was lying was useful in her role as a head of security, it was unlikely she'd ever learned how to do any spells of this difficulty. She was out of her element in this room and she knew it.

McKenzie started to close the doors behind her, flashing me one last look of annoyance before she shut them completely.

"Morgan, please take the head position," Jasmine said.

I'd been so busy watching the other woman leave, that I hadn't been paying attention to the movement in the room. Had Jasmine just asked me to take the head position? Looking around at the table, I saw that all the mages were standing around the table, Jasmine included. The only open place was at the head of the table. The position reserved for the person who would do the casting - the one who ran the whole show.

"I'm sorry, you want me to lead the ritual?" I asked.

Jasmine nodded. "You're the only one who has met the Fae we are trying to find. The connection will be strongest from you," she said.

Swallowing, I moved to the head of the table. That was true, of course. Any time you were completing a spell or a ritual that involved a specific individual, your best bet was to use whoever you had that was closest to the person. If you were trying to heal someone who was sick, having their child, or spouse cast the spell would give you the best results. I should have known that a searching spell would work the same way.

Taking a deep breath, I stood behind the tall chair. The lights in the crystal chandeliers above the center of the table flickered. Me taking the step behind the last empty chair had charged the table. There was no time for introductions, our magic was active, waiting for me to begin.

In any ritual performed in the divination room, each step had to be done with purpose. Once the thirteen were gathered, an energy or power flowed between all of us, making any magic we performed stronger than it would be on our own. Some spells could only be done with the help of other mages, that was part of why me living on my own was so unusual. A searching spell could be done by a single person, but it would get you to a general location, possibly miles away from where you really needed to be. Having all thirteen of us should get us pinpoint accuracy.

Lifting my face skyward, I closed my eyes and inhaled, knowing the others were doing the same. Silently, I prayed to the mother goddess, the protector and patron of the mages. *Please help me save my friends and the other mages. Please help me before it's too late.*

Opening my eyes, I lowered my chin, indicating that I was ready. When I pulled my chair out, the sound of twelve other chairs moving echoed around me.

Without speaking, we all sat. Hands flat on the table now, I turned and nodded to Jasmine, who was seated on my right, then reached my right hand toward her. She set her hand on top of mine, then repeated the process with the person next to her until the person on my left, a greying woman with half-moon spectacles, set her hand on top of mine.

I couldn't remember the last time I'd done a searching spell, but the principal was the same with a group as it was alone. Taking a deep breath, I whispered the incantation, surprised how easily the words rolled off my tongue. The language of magic was a fusion of several ancient tongues, the only words that remained were those we used in spell craft.

As I said the last words, a screaming pain filled my head and I squeezed the hands on either side of me. Wincing in pain, I held my breath to keep from yelling out. It felt like something had hijacked me. Wreathing tendrils wrapped their way through my insides, the same way it felt when a gifted mind reader crawled through your head. Except, this time, it was my entire body.

Clenching my teeth, I fought against the intrusion inside me. Just when I thought I was going to let my control slip, a second force joined in, pushing away the intruder. A voice echoed from inside my head. "Fight it, Morgan, fight it."

Pushing with all my might, I resisted whatever was trying to take hold of me. My eyes were open now, but all I could see was a black void. Letting go of the hands on either side of me, I slammed them on the table and let out a cry as I fought. "Get out of my head."

"Let go, Morgan," another voice filled my head now. Soothing, familiar. It startled me and for a moment, I eased up.

"James?" The words came out as if I'd said them underwater.

"Stop fighting, I'm trying to talk to you," James's voice came again.

I took a sharp breath and let go of the panic and relaxed. The pain I'd felt eased, though the slithering feeling of something invading my body didn't.

Suddenly, I felt my back hit something hard but I couldn't see anything other than the blackness around me. It seemed my body was not in my control at the moment. I should have been scared, but I was more concerned about James than my own wellbeing. If he was contacting me, I had to find out where he was. "James? Is that really you?"

"I'm sorry to do this to you," he said. "But I've been waiting for you to tap into your magic so I could reach you."

"Where are you? Chester said you're in danger," I said.

"We all are," James said. This time, I heard footsteps behind me and I turned around. A faint shimmer glowed in the distance. As I took a few steadying breaths, the form took on the shape of the handsome man I'd met in Chinatown. Bright blue eyes, tousled brown hair, tight black tee-shirt. He looked alert, healthy, safe.

"James, what is this?" I asked as relief spread through me. It seemed too good to be true, but I let myself believe that maybe everything was okay. Maybe all the bad news had been the dream and this was reality.

"We're bonded, through the favor you promised, remember?" he asked.

"That doesn't explain what's happening," I said. "Favor bonds just make it so you can't say no, they don't connect you."

"They do when you're a dragon," he said.

"So this is about cashing in your favor?" I tried not to show my disappointment. This wasn't a social call, it was all business.

"Not exactly," he said. "As soon as I ask for the favor, we'll lose this bond. I don't want that yet."

"Okay, so what's going on here, then?" I asked. "And where the hell are you? Are you safe?"

James smirked, locking his eyes on mine. It took every ounce of my willpower not to run to him.

"None of us are safe, Morgan. I've been captured and so have the others like you. I saw them," he said.

James's form was fading, the details in his face harder to make out. I had a feeling we didn't have much time left before the connection was broken. I had to get some information from him. "Tell me what to do, how to help you."

He shook his head. "I can't, or the bond will break."

"Tell me where you are," I said.

"The girls are in the old mines in Angeles National Forest. Use the Devil's Canyon trailhead."

He was almost entirely transparent now.

"Where are you?" I asked, my voice high-pitched with worry.

"Don't worry about me," he said.

Feeling desperate, I ran toward the fading wisps of his figure. "Don't say that. Tell me where you are."

As I reached my fingers toward the figure, they cut through the last remains of gray mist. He was gone, and I was alone.

All at once, the tugging in my gut vanished and I opened my eyes with a gasp. Staring up, I realized I was lying on the floor, twelve mages looking down at me.

9

"*A*re you okay?" Jasmine asked.

My head throbbed and I glanced over to see my chair on the ground. I must have fallen straight back. Sitting up, I rubbed the back of my head. "I'm okay."

"What was that?" A young male mage with freckles and red hair asked. "I've never seen anything like that."

"The spell was disrupted," Jasmine said. "But I'm not sure by what." She looked at me, as if waiting for me to explain what had just happened.

I still didn't trust the Mage Order, despite them offering to help me. They had an agenda, they wanted to find all the Dragon-Bloods in the city and I wasn't sure how noble their reasons were. While they might talk a big game at having me work with them, I couldn't be sure they didn't have something else in mind. "I had a vision."

Jasmine lifted an eyebrow. "A vision?"

It was clear she didn't believe me, but she didn't call me out. Instead, she stood, and offered her hand.

Accepting, I let her help pull me up. "I know where the missing mages are."

"What about the searching spell?" she asked. "Do you want to try again?"

I shook my head. "I don't need it. I can do this without Tavas."

"You were pretty insistent before that you had to find him," she said.

"That was before I had this information. The Oracle said he'd help me, but the future is always changing. Something must have changed," I said, half-trying to convince myself.

"What did you see?" Jasmine asked.

"A mine, in the mountains. I have to get there," I said, already moving toward the door.

"McKenzie will go with you," Jasmine said.

I stopped and turned back to Jasmine. "I don't think so. She's only going to be in the way."

"I insist," Jasmine said. "She's got talents you can use."

"The lie-detector thing?" I asked. "How is that helpful in rescuing a bunch of kidnapped mages from a cult?"

"She's a talented healer." Jasmine walked past me and opened the door. "You don't know what the state of the mages is or what they'll be like when you get there. If I remember correctly, that was your lowest score when you took your exams."

I scowled at her. While I excelled in most magic I used, healing had always been a low priority. Winning the duals I'd participated in left me with few reasons to use the spells on myself, which was how most mage kids honed their healing skills. I wanted to argue with Jasmine, to come up with a reason for not bringing a healer with me, but there wasn't a good one.

"I'm sure you need her here." It was a lousy attempt, but all I had. "Besides, you probably have some other mage you can lend me, one who isn't as valuable."

Jasmine moved over to me and I backed up against the open door. She placed her hands on the wall, on either side of my head, boxing me in. My senses prickled at the physical threat. She was trying to intimidate me. "What gives?"

The mages who had gathered in the room with us, filed through the open door, trying not to make eye contact with me as they left. As soon as they were gone, Jasmine leaned in closer to me. "One of the missing Mages is my granddaughter. She could be hurt. McKenzie is the best healer there is. You will take her with you, and you will bring my granddaughter, along with the other mages back to us. Alive and well."

"So, we're done playing good cop?" I asked.

Jasmine dropped her arms and rubbed her forehead with her fingertips. "I don't want to be anyone's cop. I just want Amaya back. She's all I have left. You of all people should understand the importance of family."

A lump rose to my throat and I saw Jasmine in a different light. If she was telling the truth, it was possible she was in as much pain as I had been when I lost my mom. Jasmine's daughter, Megan, had been a friend of my mom's, but I didn't realize she'd passed. I remembered meeting Amaya after she was born. I think I'd been around ten years old at the time. "What happened to Megan?"

"Accident a few months after your mom died." Jasmine's mouth tightened and she didn't give any more details.

I should have known. It was while I had been living in the human world. I felt for Amaya, growing up without her mom. At least she had her grandmother.

"Morgan?"

I turned away from Jasmine to see Alec and Dima waiting for me. Moving away from the door, I looked back at Jasmine. "We'll bring McKenzie, but I'm not going to babysit her. She'll have to take care of herself."

"Wait, what?" Dima said. "We're bringing that snob with us?"

"What snob?" Alec asked.

"Me," McKenzie said, hands on her hips. Somehow, she'd managed to sneak into the room. "And I don't need babysitting, I can handle myself just fine."

"Sure you can," I said, walking toward my friends. "We gotta go. No time to waste."

"Good luck," Jasmine said.

"Thanks," I said, deciding there was no point in any other conversation.

"So you found him?" Dima asked.

"Not exactly," I said. "But I know where the Mages are."

"But we need him," Dima said.

"Need who?" McKenzie said as she followed us toward the front door. "I thought you were doing a spell to find the Fae, is that what you're talking about?"

"Things changed," I said.

"But the Oracle," Alec said.

"Will you all just get in the car? I'll explain on the road." I didn't wait for them to answer me. Instead, I made my way to the car.

Someone grabbed my shoulder and I spun around to see Dima. "What gives?"

"Chester said we need the Fae. I don't like it, but you can't just go changing plans on an Oracle like that," she said.

"Look, I told you, I got what we need. We don't need Tavas." I continued to the car, stopping at the passenger side door, then turned to look at her. "You coming? Or should I drive myself?"

"This isn't a good idea," Dima said, making her way to the driver's side. "I have a bad feeling. Something's not right."

"What about this would make you feel right?" I asked. "We're chasing down some crazy cult that has kidnapped a bunch of mages with the intention of killing them. We don't know why they want to kill them or how they'll do it or even if they are keeping them safe right now. All we know is that they need us."

"I just think maybe we should listen to the Oracle, that's all," Dima said. "I mean, he did tell us to find Tavas. And now we're skipping it."

"I told you, it's fine," I said.

"Maybe this isn't such a good idea," McKenzie said.

"You're welcome to stay here," I said. "Come on, Dima, Alec. Let's go."

"I can't believe I'm going to say this, but the mage is right," Dima said. "Something happened and you're not telling us."

"You want to know what happened?" I shouted. "James found me. He told me exactly where he and the rest of the Dragon Mages are. I know the time is limited, we have to get to them."

"Who is James?" McKenzie asked.

"A friend of Morgan's," Dima answered for me.

"How did he come to you while you were in the middle of a spell?" McKenzie asked, her words slow, her brows pressed together in concern. "That shouldn't be possible."

"He said it was dragon magic," I said.

"It's because of that thing he did to you, isn't it?" Alec said.

"Alec, stay out of this," I said.

"What thing, Morgan?" Dima asked.

"Something about a favor," Alec said.

"You're favor-bound to a dragon?" Dima asked. "Oh, that's going to end well."

"He didn't use the favor," I said. "He just gave me the location to where the mages were being kept."

"That makes it even more important to find Tavas," Dima said.

"He told you where the mages were?" McKenzie asked.

"Yes, how many times do I have to say it?" I asked, frustration twisting inside me. Pulling the door handle, I opened the door. "I'm leaving. Is anyone coming with me?"

McKenzie walked to the car, opening the door behind mine.

"I'm with you." She didn't look like she was happy about it. "We need to help those mages."

"Finally," I said.

"I sure hope you know what you're doing," Dima said, opening her door.

Alec walked to the car silently. McKenzie moved over and he slid into the seat behind me.

"Let's go," I said.

10

When we neared the edge of Realm's Gate, I could feel something that wasn't quite right. Squinting ahead, I tried to pinpoint the cause of my unease. The sun was low in the sky as the afternoon neared its end. We'd wasted so much time already.

"Where's the ward?" Dima asked.

That was it. The usual energy I felt from the ward was missing. It was like there was a missing charge from the air. Fear and guilt tumbled around me. This was my fault. The dragon fire must have damaged it beyond repair. "I don't see it."

"Is that how the Dragon- Bloods got in? I mean, if they weren't locals, they'd have been kept outside unless there was someone on the inside, right?" Alec said.

"I'm sure there was help on the inside. After all, Tavas was here," I said.

"Yeah, but the Oracle said he didn't do it," Dima said. "Remember?"

I took a deep breath and pressed my lips together, refusing to answer her statement. Tavas might not be directly responsible, but I wasn't ready to forgive him for his involvement in all of this. Whatever was going on, whoever the mastermind behind all of it was, I knew that Tavas was involved. He might not have put the stake through Jimmy's heart, but he was involved.

The car passed through the place the ward should be and a chill ran through me. It was unnerving. Like walking through a thunderstorm without feeling the electric charge to the air.

"You think they know it's down?" Alec asked.

"I'm sure they're already working on it," Dima said.

"They don't know yet," McKenzie said.

I turned to look at her in the back seat. I'd almost forgotten she was there. "How do you figure?"

"The Mage Order keeps that thing working," she said. "If it goes down, they'd call us. Unless someone is not making the call on purpose."

"Who makes the call?" Alec asked.

"Not sure," McKenzie said, picking up her phone. She started tapping away at the screen, then looked up at me. "I've let Jasmine know. They'll be able to fix it."

She glanced back down at her phone, mouth drawing into a frown. She tapped at the screen again.

"What is it?" I asked.

"No service," she said. "That's weird. You have service?"

I pulled my phone out of my pocket and glanced down at the little bars on the top. It was a new phone and should have better reception than my old one. My brow furrowed. No service. I'd never lost service in the woods outside of Realm's Gate before. "Maybe a cell tower is down or something?"

"Check mine." Dima handed me her phone, keeping her eyes on the road.

I looked down at it. Same thing. No bars, no service. "Nothing."

"How about you, little vamp?" McKenzie said.

"They took mine when they threw me in the daylight cells. Haven't gotten a new one yet," he said.

"Well, looks like we're going to have to count on someone from Realm's Gate to let the Mages know," I said. There was no way I was going to let Dima turn the car around. We were on a race against time and every second we wasted was another second that the other dragon mages and James were potentially being tortured or starved or worse.

"Someone will see it soon," McKenzie said.

I wasn't sure if she was talking to herself or to us, so I ignored her. Right now, I wasn't especially worried about anyone inside of Realm's Gate. Marco and the other vampires I called my friends could take care of themselves just fine.

I opened the glove box and started digging.

"What are you looking for?" Dima asked.

"Got a map in here? Without service, we aren't exactly going to be able to use the GPS on our phones."

"Good point," she said. "But, no. I don't have a map. I have a phone."

"Do gas stations still sell maps?" Alec asked.

"Oh no," I said. "We are not going to visit Chester."

"There are other gas stations," he said.

"Fine, yes, first gas station we see, we stop and find a map," I said.

The car fell silent as Dima drove through the dark woods. I stared out the window, watching the clouds as we flew past them. The memory of James speaking to me in the dark nothingness flashed into my mind. His eyes had seemed sharp, focused, alert. He didn't seem to be in pain. I hoped that meant he was safe and unharmed. I hoped it meant all the missing people were safe and unharmed.

The trees thinned as we drove along the winding road and I

could tell that we were nearing the end of the national forest, nearing the highway and civilization, and nearby cities.

Dima accelerated as we joined the rush of bright lights speeding down the freeway. Despite the speed we traveled at now, the interior of the car seemed to be frozen in time. Everyone too lost in their own thoughts. Absentmindedly, I checked my phone again. "Still no signal." I glanced at Dima's phone, still in my lap. "On either phone."

"That's weird," Dima said.

"Mine's dead," McKenzie said. "I thought I charged it before we left, but I must not have."

"Gas station at the next exit," I said.

The blinker clicked as Dima changed lanes. She slowed as she left the freeway and we pulled into a gas station. The sign above the store was dark, but the interior lights glowed warm and bright. Dima pulled into a parking place and turned off the engine. "Anyone need anything?"

"I'll come in with you," I said.

"Then I'm going, too," McKenzie said.

I turned and glanced back at Alec.

"Well, shit, if you're all going, guess I'm in," he said, opening the door next to him.

We all walked toward the gas station and I was surprised to find myself smiling as I thought about my first encounter with Chester. There was no way I'd run into anything odd at this gas station. I'd been to human gas stations hundreds of times and Chester was the first unusual thing I'd ever run into.

Alec opened the door, then stood back, holding it for the rest of us. "Ladies first."

Dima and McKenzie walked in, and I held back for a moment with Alec. "You don't think I'm making a mistake, do you?"

"Are you talking about Tavas?" he asked.

I nodded.

"Honestly, I don't know. But if there's a way to avoid being around that guy, I think it's a good idea." He smiled at me.

"Thanks," I said as I stepped over the threshold. I glanced toward the counter where the checker should be working. It was empty. Stopping right in front of the door, I looked around the small store. We seemed to be the only people here. Goosebumps rose on my arms.

Alec bumped into me. "Hey, why'd you stop?"

Turning around, I pushed him back out the door. "Go back to the car, something's not right."

"You don't have to tell me twice." He turned and left.

"Dima, McKenzie, we need to go, now." I said the words quietly, but the store was small. They should have heard me. Instead, there was no response.

Shit. Moving from the semi-safety of the door, I walked across the front of the store, pacing the counter. "Where'd you two go?"

There were only six aisles, and as I walked by them, I didn't see either woman. How had they disappeared in the few seconds I was talking to Alec?

The sound of something metallic dropping, like coins against the ground, came from a narrow hallway to the left of the counter. Slowly, I made my way toward the hallway.

This is what I got for feeling so sure that nothing bad could come from a gas station. Now I really missed Chester.

Staying to the side, I peeked around the corner of the hall, trying not to give myself away in case there was something terrible hiding down there. Both McKenzie and Dima were standing in the hallway, fixed in place. My first instinct was to call out to them, but before I could, I noticed a shimmer in front of them. There was magic hiding here. Well-masked, extremely well-hidden magic. I hadn't even sensed it. Just like Chester's gas station, there was something here that was preventing me from getting a good read.

Before whatever was there could see me, I flattened myself against the wall. What was I going to do? There was a monster of some sort hiding behind magic I didn't know anything about. It would really help to have someone who knew what the fuck they were doing here. And the one person who was supposed to be protecting us on this trip was frozen next to Dima. My nose crinkled. I knew McKenzie would be more trouble than she was worth.

Slowly, I blew out a breath and tried to think of a plan. There had to be something in my magic arsenal that could at least drop the guise the monster was hiding behind. Why had I stopped practicing after my mom died? A tingle spread up my arms at the thought of my mother. She'd left that journal for me. Magic I could learn to use because of the dragon blood inside me. But there wasn't time to learn how to use new magic now. I had to use something I already knew.

The only new thing I'd mastered, was to call to fire without a spell. And the fire I made now wasn't mage fire. A smile spread on my lips. I could make dragon fire, which had the ability to render magic useless. Whatever it was that was hiding back there, wouldn't be hiding for long.

Hoping I wasn't making a huge mistake, I called out to my friends from my safety against the wall. If I could bring whatever it was to me, maybe it would release them. "Dima, McKenzie, you guys okay?"

No response.

"You two need some help?" I asked.

This time, I felt a change in the air. It moved near me, heavier than it should be. For a fraction of a second, I caught a glimmer of something that reminded me of the wards around Realm's Gate. The lights above us flickered, the florescent buzzing ceasing for a moment, then returning brighter and louder than before. The smell of sulfur filled the air and I could taste the rotten egg scent on my tongue.

I wasn't sure what kind of creature would have a signature like that. It wasn't anything I'd sensed before, but I had a feeling it wasn't good. Not wanting to wait to find out if it was going to paralyze me the way it had my friends, I thought about fire. The scent of sulfur helping fuel my thoughts as I imagined brimstone and blazing flames.

Fire spread from my fingertips to my elbows. Gathering the flames, I formed them into a sphere. All the while, scanning the empty space in front of me, waiting for the unseen monster to reveal itself.

11

*M*y heart thundered in my chest and I ignored the prickle of fear that made the hair on the back of my neck rise. Pushing away the dark thought and negativity that were rising inside me, I waited, hoping I'd be able to strike before the creature took his blow at me.

Just as a nervous bead of sweat slid down my face, I caught a glimpse of a shimmer out of the corner of my eye.

Faster than I thought possible, I knelt down, twisting toward the shimmer, and launched the ball of flame. For a terrible moment, I thought I'd missed as it struck a shelf of potato chips. Then, the flames spread, and the shimmer returned like an iridescent ripple that expanded from thin air.

My breath caught in my chest as the core of the ripple revealed a fuzzy black head, with hundreds of tiny bead-like eyes blinking at me. The creature hissed, showing its fangs and began to scurry toward me, eight long legs clicking against the tile floor.

I found myself facing off against a giant spider, and for a moment, I stood open-mouthed in terror. A scream sounded from somewhere behind me, or maybe inside me, and I lunged out of the way just in time to avoid the snapping of its jaws. Falling to my side, I rolled away, then pushed up to standing as fast as I could. The fire on my hands was gone and I wasn't sure if it would even be effective against whatever this thing was. "I did not sign up for this!"

Igniting the flames again, faster this time, I threw another fireball at the creature. It reared up on its back legs and let out a shriek that made me wince in pain. Nails on the chalkboard was nothing compared to this.

It charged and I looked around desperate to find something to stab it with. Not seeing anything, I had a choice to make. Run through the door, hoping it would follow me, or make my stand. Shit. Knowing I was about to do something really stupid, I ignored my intuition telling me to flee. Ducking down, I moved closer to the beast, then swerved, taking my chances running under its huge belly between its spindly legs.

The spider was slow to register my movement and I tore away from it, running down the back aisle of the store, looking for a weapon.

Clicking legs sounded behind me and I held my breath as I grabbed a can of charcoal fire starter off of the shelf. The cap seemed to be stuck and I twisted, trying to break the child-proof seal.

With a screech and a rattle, the spider stopped in front of me, its jaws open, ready to descend. I backed up, still twisting the lid. It didn't budge. This had been a stupid idea. I was going to get eaten by a massive spider. Of all the ways I could die, this was not the one I expected.

Suddenly, I got the top of the bottle off and I yelled a battle cry as I squirted the liquid at the creature. It hissed and backed up a few paces. Once the fluid was gone, I tossed the bottle to the side and the spider blinked its eyes at me, then leaned forward as if it were ready to pounce.

"Oh no you don't," I said, thinking of a roaring bonfire. The dragon fire came to me easily, heat rising up to my face, filling me with resolve. Extending my arms out in front of me, I aimed at the spider, willing the flames to fly forward. I moved on instinct, and to my great surprise, the fire obliged my internal command. An arc of heat roared toward the creature and as soon as the flames touched, it ignited in a ball of orange flames. Heat expanded with the explosion, making me close my eyes against the sudden increase in temperature. The smell of burning hair and gasoline filled my nostrils.

The beast let out one of those wince-inducing screeches. This time, I relished the noise. It was the sound of pain. Of a monster burning alive.

The spider folded in on itself, crumpling to the ground like an ordinary house spider that had been crushed by a boot. Breathing heavy, I watched it shrivel up under the flames.

"Morgan?"

The sound of someone calling my name broke me of my trance and I looked around, realizing for the first time that while I had succeeded in killing the spider, I had also set fire to the store.

A hand grabbed my arm and I turned to see Alec. "What the fuck were you thinking? The whole place is going to go if we don't get out of here."

"Did you not see the giant spider?" I asked.

He lifted a skeptical eyebrow. "Giant spider?"

I grabbed his chin and turned it toward the burning pile of goo on the ground. One of the massive legs twitched as the carcass crumbled.

Alec jumped back, away from the beast, letting out a disgusted cry. "Good thinking on the fire. But now, it's time to go."

Black clouds filled the small convenience store and I

coughed, waving it away with my still smoking hands. Closing my hands into fists, I tried to quench the smoke coming from me. My pulse raced. While I focused on killing the spider, I didn't think about how dangerous it would be to have this much fire at a gas station. "We have to get Dima and McKenzie."

Tears streamed down my cheeks as the fumes burned my eyes and throat. Without waiting for Alec, I tugged at his shirt and dragged him down the aisle, away from the smoldering corpse of the arachnid. We walked up the next aisle and I squinted through the gray clouds as I made my way to the hallway.

McKenzie and Dima were still standing there, unmoving. For the first time, I noticed the webbing wrapped around them. I grabbed at it, pulling it away as best I could but all it did was stick to my hands.

"We have to get out of here," Alec said. He wrapped his arms around both women and picked them up, hoisting them over his shoulders like duffle bags. Their heads bounced as he walked with them.

I pushed my way in front of Alec and helped guide him to the door, then held it open for him to pass through. He moved slower than usual, but I didn't think it was from the strain of carrying them. He seemed to be more concerned about making sure they were safe and weren't bobbing too much.

Alec leaned them against the hood of the car. "Keys?"

"Dima had them," I said.

The whole store was ablaze now. We didn't have long until a spark would find its way to the pumps. Frantic, I tore at the sticky webbing around Dima's hands. My heart nearly leapt from my chest when I felt the familiar metal keyring. Tugging it, I managed to break it free from her hand. "Got them!"

Alec already had McKenzie in the back of the car. Quickly, he grabbed Dima. "Drive."

As he shoved Dima in the back seat, I revved up the engine. As soon as Alec closed the passenger door behind him, I gunned it.

"You didn't happen to grab a map, did you?" Alec asked.

I looked over at him as I accelerated onto the freeway. "Seriously? You're asking me about the map?"

"Would you rather I ask you how the hell a giant spider got into a human gas station?" he asked.

I gripped the wheel tighter. "I'm not even sure that was a spider."

"Did it have eight legs?" he asked.

I glared at him as I took the next exit. "I didn't count them, if that's what you're asking."

"That's not what I meant," he said.

"I know what you meant," I said. "It looked like a spider, but I don't know if it was something else. Some other kind of creature. But I don't think that's what matters right now."

I slowed down, and pulled into an empty parking lot, taking the space furthest from the road, then stopped the car. "Right now, we have to help Dima."

"And McKenzie," Alec added.

"Sure, her too," I said.

12

*A*lec and I opened the back doors of the car. "Feel for a pulse," I said, touching my fingers to the neck of the wrapped body closest to me. It was McKenzie and while I didn't want her here, I wasn't keen on the idea of her dying by giant spider while chasing down the Dragon-Bloods. I knew I hadn't started this whole thing in motion, but it all went back to me. If not for me, the wild dragon wouldn't have escaped, and Jimmy might even still be alive. His only crime was employing me.

Adjusting my position, I moved my fingers along McKenzie's neck, hoping to find a sign of life. While I pressed into her neck, I looked up at Alec. The weak light on the roof of the car cast dark shadows on his pale face. He looked tired.

Then, I felt it, a faint throbbing under my fingertips. "She's got a pulse." I pulled my hand away and leaned over McKenzie's prone form. "Please tell me you found one on Dima."

He looked like he was holding his breath, despite the fact that he didn't need to breathe. Finally, he looked up at me and nodded. "It's there, it's weak, but it's there."

I let out a breath of relief. "Thank the gods. Now, we just have to figure out how to get this stuff off of them and wake them up."

"Hey, Morgan?" Alec asked.

"Yeah?"

"Is there a reason why Dima's tongue would be purple. I mean, is that a siren thing?" he asked.

My blood ran cold and I turned McKenzie's head toward me, harder than I should have, and pried her mouth open. Her tongue was purple, too. "Shit."

"What is it?" Alec asked.

"They've been poisoned. The spider must have bit them or stung them. They were injected with something." I backed up and stood outside the car, pressing my palms to my forehead. We'd learned about this in our magic studies as kids. Something about treating poison. At the time, it had seemed so important and I, like the other mage children in my class, had paid close attention.

Years passed, and I never had reason to use the magic associated with treating magical poisons. So I didn't worry about it, and I moved on to the Realm's Gate high school, focusing on the flashier, more interesting magical studies. The healing arts never seemed important. I could treat burns, scratches, cuts, the basics. But those didn't even require magic to heal if they were minor. Since nobody had ever actually been poisoned, I hadn't worried about it. Chalked it up to overly cautious elders who wanted to scare us into behaving.

"How do we fix it?" Alec asked as he neared me.

I dropped my hands to my sides in frustration. "I'm not sure. I know there's something I can do, a spell, I just don't remember it."

Pulling my phone out of my pocket, I checked for service. It was still down. Frowning, I started to pace in a small circle.

I thought back to the lessons from my childhood. Fennel. I stopped walking, the spell was coming back to me. "We need to find fennel. I think I remember the spell."

I opened the car door and hopped into the driver's seat.

Alec took the passenger seat next to me, then shut the door behind him. "Fennel? Like the seed they add to Italian food?"

I started the car and pulled away from the parking lot. "Not the seed, we need the whole bulb. Or powdered fennel, that would be best. If we could find a metaphysical store, we might get lucky. Sometimes they keep supplies for spells in the back of those shops."

"So what, we drive till we find a place to buy this stuff?" he asked.

"I guess so, I don't know what else we can do."

"How much time do we have?" he asked.

"Minutes, hours, I don't know," I said, a heavy weight resting in the pit of my stomach. We were supposed to be on our way to save James, Lyla, and the other missing dragon mages. Instead, I was now on a side quest to save the rescuers.

"I can make a call," Alec said.

"Phones are dead," I said. "Besides, who would you call?"

"Some of the local guys owe me. Just find me a gas station or something, I can ask to use their phone."

"No more gas stations," I said, eyeing the sign ahead of us. The next exit was in twelve miles, along with a slew of fast food restaurants. "We can try one of the food places."

We drove in silence as I wondered what local guy Alec would call. Was it another vampire? Whoever it was, I was guessing it was his past employer. Whoever he'd worked for before Jimmy. Was there vampire organized crime in the human world, too?

"So do you just give them the fennel and they're good?" Alec asked. It seemed that while I had been wondering about his past, he was wondering about magic.

"Not quite," I said. "I'll have to cast a spell. Fennel is just part of it."

"I thought you were an ex-mage. All I've ever seen you do is light things on fire," Alec said.

The ghost of a smile crossed my lips. I hadn't considered the fact that every time I'd used magic in front of Alec, it had been to use fire. Mage fire, or maybe even dragon fire in the Dizzy Dragon the night I threatened Dima. My brow furrowed as I remembered how the flames had seemed to come of their own accord.

My hands felt hot and I pulled them off the steering wheel with a gasp. The car swerved into the next lane.

Alec grabbed the wheel and righted us. Thankfully we were alone on the highway. "What happened?"

With a deep breath, I thought about snow, cold, ice cubes floating in a cold drink. The heat eased and relief washed through me. I had to get this thing under control. Taking back the wheel, I glanced at Alec. "Thanks."

"You okay? Need me to drive?"

"I'm okay." Hands shaking, I gripped the wheel tighter and held the feeling of cold in my head.

"What the hell was that?" he asked. "Looked like you touched something hot."

My eyes widened in surprise. That was an astute observation. "I kind of did."

"What, the steering wheel heated up?" he asked.

"No, I did." I paused, waiting for him to say something, but he remained silent. "I guess that's part of the whole dragon blood thing. I can call fire without a spell. I just have to think about it and it comes."

"Wow." He stared straight ahead, looking out the windshield.

"I know," I said. "James said I'd have to learn how to control it. He implied that he could help me learn."

"So it's not just the fact that you have a thing for him," Alec said. "It's the whole *he's a dragon* thing. It's so weird. I still can't believe that you're part dragon."

"Yeah, it's weird for me, too." No longer shaking, I felt like I had regained control of myself, but I wondered how long it would be before I forgot myself again. Part of me wanted to explain to Alec that it was more than just needing a teacher. There was something in me that was drawn to James. I wasn't sure if it was because we shared the connection of being dragons. I wasn't sure if it was simply because of his looks. Either option scared me. I was either going mad, feeling a pull to someone I barely knew, or I was more vain than I thought.

"Then there's the favor," Alec added.

"There is that." I thought about it. Maybe that's all it was. The pull to James. Maybe it was the favor I owed him. Was that how it worked when someone was favor-bound? "But he hasn't asked it yet."

"Didn't he tell you where they were hiding?" Alec asked.

"He did, but he didn't ask me to do anything about it," I said. "He said he didn't want to use it because the connection would break once he does."

"Got it," Alec said.

We drove past a green sign that let us know our exit was coming up. I flipped the blinker on and got into the exit lane. "Here's hoping there's no random monsters waiting for us at the Taco Bell."

"You can't tell me you think that was random," Alec said.

"Good point." I pressed down on the brakes, slowing the car. It made zero sense for a spider monster, or whatever that thing was to be at that gas station. "But if it wasn't random, how did it know we'd be there?"

"No idea, but I'd guess someone sent it," Alec said. "Someone knows you're looking for the missing mages and they don't want you to succeed. Honestly, if you'd gone in alone, or if you'd gone in at the same time as the other two, you'd probably be in the same state as them."

I swallowed against a lump in my throat. In the moment, I hadn't stopped to think about what the creature was doing there or what could have happened. And Alec's point made sense. Besides the mage order, who knew I was looking for the dragon mages?

Pulling into a parking spot in front of the doors, I put the car in park. Then, I reached around the seat and felt for a pulse on Lyla's neck. It was still weak, but she was hanging on. I looked over at Alec. "Whoever you're going to call, they better be able to help us find the fennel powder quick."

He opened the door. "They will." Then he stepped out of the car. Before he closed the door, he ducked down to look at me. "If I'm not back in five minutes, please come in and kill whoever is trying to eat me."

"You got it," I said, trying to make light of the situation. Internally, anxiety bubbled inside me and I really hoped we had better luck headed our way.

13

Tapping a rhythm on the wheel, I waited for Alec. He'd been in there a while and I was starting to get nervous. "Okay, Alec, you have thirty seconds." I said the words aloud, even though nobody would be able to respond to me.

I started counting. Just as I got to twenty-seven, the door opened, and Alec came jogging out. He held a piece of paper in his hand. Opening the door, he plopped into the seat. "Got it. There's a witch not far from here. She can help us."

My nose wrinkled. Witches were some of my least favorite people. They were humans who had learned to use magic. Usually just healing potions, communicating with the dead, or sending away demons. They had their uses for humans, for sure, but they weren't anything compared to the magic a mage could wield. They couldn't do anything elemental, no making fire from thin air or anything like that. It wasn't that I begrudged what they did, it was the fact that they so often thought themselves superior to others. And they tended to play up their "witchy-ness" by dressing oddly or acting out how they thought a witch should be. It made me uncomfortable.

"Next town over," Alec said. "They said we can follow this

frontage road and we'll hit a town center. We turn off of main, onto Second Avenue, then...Why aren't you driving?"

Shaking away my prejudice, I moved the car into reverse and pulled out of the spot. Now wasn't the time for me to care about what this witch would be like. We needed the fennel power. "You say she's got the powder for sure?"

Alec nodded. "Yes, and she's expecting us."

"This some old girlfriend or something?" I asked.

"Not mine, but I think she dated my friend," Alec said.

"The person you called?" I asked.

"Yeah," Alec said. He didn't offer any more information about his contact or how he was able to find a witch who just happened to have the item we needed.

Part of me was suspicious. After all, Tavas had seemed like a friend right up until the point he stabbed me in the back. And Alec hadn't gone into the gas station with the rest of us.

I glanced at the silent vampire and wished, for the first time in my life, that I could read minds. "Is there anything we should be prepared for?"

"What do you mean?"

"I mean, this friend, this witch, do you trust them? Are they connected to anyone inside Realm's Gate?" I asked.

He shook his head. "No, not at all. And yes, I trust my friend and he said she was a friend."

I thought about Dima and her weakened state. She didn't have long before the poison would be irreversible. My choices were to either trust Alec, who hadn't ever given me reason not to, or take my chances driving around until I found some fennel powder.

Pressing down on the gas, I sped down the frontage road. "Main Street to Second Avenue?"

"That's right." He glanced at the paper in his hands. "Then we turn on Maple Place and it's the third house on the right."

Hoping that I was trusting the right person, I continued down the road. Guilt and fear mingled inside me. I shouldn't be doubting Alec, but it was difficult to blindly trust after everything that happened in the last few days. I wondered if this was how James felt all the time. He didn't even believe I was who I said I was, even after Marco called him and gave him a heads-up. It was a terrible way to live. My heart ached for James. How long had he been alone in that house, worrying that someone was after him? The worst part was, that he was right. They were after him. And they found him because he shifted to protect me.

Now, two more people were in danger because of me. When this was over, I was going to need to lock myself up somewhere and stop causing trouble. I wondered if James would let me crash at his place. I could disappear with him for a while.

"Turn here!" Alec shouted.

With a start, I realized I'd stopped paying attention to where I was. Pulling a tight last-minute turn, I swerved onto Main Street. Thankfully, it was just as empty as the highway had been. "Sorry."

"It's fine, just keep an eye out for Second," Alec said.

We drove down a narrow street lined with small shops and buildings with weathered looking brick. Several of them had the false store fronts that looked right out of an old western movie. My senses tingled as I was bombarded with magic. It felt similar to the way Realm's Gate felt with all of the different creatures living together. The only thing that could explain it was if this town was like home, with more than just a few citizens who had magical signatures. "What is this place?"

"My friend called it *Nowhere*. But I don't know what that means, exactly."

The magic pulsed through me and I felt my power rise. There was an energy here that was different, but I couldn't place what it was. All I knew was that I felt like everything was ampli-

fied. I hoped it didn't mean that the venom inside my friends
was picking up pace, too.

A faded brown street sign ahead read *Second Ave.* I turned
onto a narrow tree-lined street. Grass and manicured flower
beds filled the space between the road and the honest-to-god
white picket fences that surrounded the little single story pastel
houses. Main Street might have looked like the old west, but this
was right out of the 1950's. I was almost surprised to see it
in color.

That's when I noticed that we weren't just the only car
driving down the road, we were the only car, period. "There's no
cars parked on the street."

"It's weird, isn't it?" Alec said. "After so many years living in
the city, I didn't have any idea how quiet small towns could be."

My skin prickled uncomfortably. There was nothing about
this place that I liked. The sooner we could get out of here, the
better.

"Turn there," Alec pointed and I turned to the right, onto
another pristine white-picket fenced street. These houses were
larger than the last street, most of them more modern looking
with three-car garages and two levels. The lack of cars persisted,
but at least these houses had space to store them away.

I tried to shake the discomfort I was feeling. Tried telling
myself it was just like Alec said, a small town. What did I know
about small towns, anyway? For all I knew, it was totally normal
to see no signs of human or animal life after dark.

"There," Alec pointed to a gray house with a circular
driveway.

I turned onto the driveway, overly aware of the fact that this
house would be the only one with a car parked in front of it.

"Let me go ask for her," Alec said. "Then I'll come back
for you."

Alec opened the door and I reached across, grabbing his arm. He stopped and looked back at me.

I wanted to ask him if he was telling me the truth, if he was still on my side. Instead, I dropped my arm and said, "Hurry."

Killing the engine seemed like the right thing to do. The noise and light from the car would draw attention. So I sat, feeling the chill in the night air without the heater running, and waiting as the seconds dragged by.

Finally, the garage door in front of us opened. Alec stood inside with a woman who must be the witch. She wore a long black dress, and several scarves hung around her neck, forming a layer of color under a collection of large amulets on long chains. Her red hair fell in loose ringlets around her pale face. She looked like she was trying too hard to dress the part. I sighed.

Alec waved me in to the garage so I started the engine and pulled the car in, hoping I wasn't making a terrible mistake, and feeling equal parts guilty and nervous. I hated that I was doubting Alec, but I knew I'd feel better once this was over with and we could get back to saving James and Lyla.

As soon as the car was inside, the door lowered behind me. I turned the engine off again and opened the car door, stepping out onto the hard cement ground.

To my surprise, my car was the only one in the garage. Did they even have cars here at all?

The red-haired woman, who I was guessing was the witch we came to see, walked over toward me. "You must be Morgan."

"I am," I said, "and you are?"

"They call me Moonbeam," she said with an airy lilt to her voice.

It was almost painful maintaining a straight-faced reaction to her name. It was just going to be one of those nights.

"We were told you have fennel powder?" I asked, ready to get this over with and leave this creepy town.

"I do," she said. "It's one of my usual stock. It comes in so handy," she said with a smile.

It was almost like she wanted me to agree with her, or congratulate her or somehow validate her. But I couldn't bring myself to do that. Fennel powder was useful against poisons, but other than that, I couldn't think of another reason I'd ever need it. Maybe they had a rattlesnake problem in Nowhere, California. "I hate to do this, Moonbeam," I swallowed, having a hard time believing I was saying that name out loud, "but can we get that powder and get going? We're running short on time."

She lifted her hands in the air, palms out, then tossed her head back, then closed her eyes. She stood there unmoving.

I looked at Alec. "What's she doing?"

"I have no idea," he said.

"I'm communicating with the goddess," Moonbeam said. "I have to make sure your friends are meant to live. If we revive them, and this was their fate, it will upset the balance."

"You have got to be kidding me," I said. "Listen, isn't the fact that we're here in time to cure them answer enough? If they weren't meant to be cured, we wouldn't have been able to reach you, right?"

She dropped her arms and righted her head. Staring at me, she blinked a few times as if processing what I just said. Was she trying to find error in my logic?

"The goddess speaks to me," she said. "It's why they let me live here, even though I am not magic born, like you. I'm merely a human who was gifted with magic. In some ways, that makes what I can do even more significant that what you can do. My powers came from the gods themselves."

"I'm very happy for you," I said. "Now, are you going to help us?"

"I don't know if I can, the goddess seems to think you need to be taught a lesson." She crossed her arms over her chest.

This woman was standing between life and death for my friends. I didn't know her, I didn't owe her anything. And I did not like her. Not even a little bit. If she wasn't going to cooperate, maybe it was time for some good-cop, bad-cop. I had a feeling Alec would play nice, which meant it was up to me to be the bad-cop. "Alec, it's been a while since you've eaten, right?"

"Morgan, just calm down, I'm sure Moonbeam wants to help us, right?" Alec said.

The witch turned to Alec. "You can't harm me, anyway. I was granted eternal life."

"Right," I said. "Okay, I'm over this. Please show us where the powder is or I'll test out your eternal life theory."

My temperature rose, and I could feel the fire inside me vibrating, begging for release. I focused on it. With a grin, I lowered my hands, palms facing the unhelpful witch. One second, my hands were bare, the next a rush of fire spread from my fingertips to my elbows.

The witch's eyes widened. "What are you?"

Behind me, I heard the sound of the garage door opening and I glanced behind me for a moment, just in time to see a group of hunters staring back at me.

14

I tensed as I squeezed my hands into fists. Scanning the scowling faces in front of me, I did a quick count. There were four men dressed in the typical hunter style. Leather jackets over worn jeans, stakes and other unusual weapons dangling off their belts. I did a double take. These weren't mage hunters, they were vampire hunters.

Before I could explain anything, I moved in front of Alec protectively. I'd lost him once before to a group of hunters and I wasn't going to let it happen again. "What's the meaning of this?"

Moonbeam walked over to the group, glancing back at me as she moved. Her black dress swept behind her as she walked and for the first time I realized it had to be made of a lightweight fabric, maybe silk. Who wears a long, black silk dress around the house?

"Sorry, little mage, I called them here." She stopped when she reached the hunters and turned back around so all five people were staring back at us. "You see, we don't like outsiders here in Nowhere. It's our little haven. Not the anarchy of the human world or the free-for-all that you find in Realm's Gate.

Don't get me wrong, we're open to all kinds here, just not *his* kind."

Moonbeam lifted her chin to Alec. "No vampires allowed."

My brow furrowed. "What? You knew he was coming. It was set up by a friend of his. You should have told us not to come."

Alec stepped out from behind me. "We're not staying. We just want to help our friends. Then we'll be gone. That's it."

"I'd like to help you, really I would. I feel bad for the young ladies in the car. And had you come on your own, little mage, I probably would have healed your friends for you."

If I wasn't already angry at the red-head smiling at me, this would be my breaking point. "First of all, stop calling me little mage. Second, I don't need you to heal my friends, I just need some fennel powder. That's it. Either you have it, or you don't."

"Oh, I have it," she said. "But I wouldn't ever give it to someone who associates freely with a vampire. Their kind is an abomination against the goddess. She's the only one who should be giving eternal life."

I could feel the heat rising inside me and was worried I was going to lose control. While I could easily take down the witch, I wasn't sure if I could handle four hunters on my own. And I wasn't exactly keen on the idea of killing five people, even if they were standing in my way. "Hey, I'm sorry some vampire wronged you in the past," I said. "But you're really going to let two innocent non-vampires die over it?"

"This is your one chance, you can all leave now, or you'll be formally charged with bringing a vampire into Nowhere without permission," she said.

"Let's just go, Morgan," Alec said. "We can find it somewhere close, I bet."

I narrowed my eyes, looking at each of the hunters standing behind the witch. They hadn't moved a muscle since the open garage door revealed them. In fact, now that I was looking closer,

I realized that all of them looked exactly the same. Under my breath, I whispered a detection spell. The basic spell I used to find magical objects at estate sales also worked to detect the magic in beings. There was no magical signature coming from any of the gathered figures. Either they were all human, or they weren't actually there. My money was on the latter.

A smile spread across my lips. "Yeah, I don't think that's going to happen."

For a fraction of a second, the witch's expression gave her away, as just the slightest flicker of panic flashed in her eyes. Then she pursed her lips, an attempt to regain control of the situation. "Fine. Have it your way."

"Morgan?" Alec said, shifting closer to me.

I put my arm out to signal for him to stop. "You're good for a witch, I'll give you that. But you're no match for someone with real magic."

Her upper lip curled. "Real magic? You think you're so special. Born with the gift. It just means you had it easy." She extended her arms up, and the hunters charged, weapons drawn.

Alec yelled and tried to drag me toward the car. I held my ground, waiting for her illusions to come crashing down around her.

The hunters were right in front of us, matching gray eyes, matching stakes raised in each man's right hand. At this distance, I could see through them, and I knew I'd been right.

"What the?" Alec asked as the hunters ran right through us, vanishing in a cloud of smoke.

"Illusions," I said. "None of it was real."

Moonbeam looked pissed. "I'm still not helping you."

With a sigh, I whispered another spell. It was bad enough that I had to tap into my past to do a healing spell I didn't want to do. Now, she was making me think up non-lethal magic I could use to keep her quiet while I searched her house. She wouldn't be able to see the tendrils that stretched from my fingertips, she didn't have the gift of seeing magic, which is part of what seemed to be making her so angry at me.

The invisible strings wrapped around her, binding her arms to her body. She stiffened and struggled, trying to break free of her bonds. "What are you doing to me?"

I glared at her. "Real magic. Not illusions. Now tell me, do you or do you not have fennel powder?"

Moonbeam pressed her lips together and stared at me defiantly.

Lifting an eyebrow, I smiled. "You want to play, then?"

The fire came with ease this time. It was as if it had been simmering dormant under my skin, waiting to come out. Slowly, I approached, getting a sick sense of satisfaction from the look of terror mingling with the reflection of the flames in her eyes.

"We can just go inside and look," Alec said.

"I'm not wasting any more time on this," I said, pausing in front of her. "If my friends die, I will kill you."

I wasn't sure if the words were a lie or not. At this point, an unfamiliar adrenaline rushed through me, fueling the intense anger I felt toward this witch.

She swallowed. "In my pantry in the kitchen. I keep herbs labeled in bags and jars. There should be some in there."

I turned to Alec but he was already through the door.

"You better hope he finds some," I said.

"Got it," Alec jumped over the steps that led to the garage door and stretched out a hand to me. "You going to turn the fire off or you want to toast this stuff first?"

Squeezing my fingers to my palms, I extinguished the flames, then I took the jar of powder from Alec.

"What are you?" Moonbeam asked. "I've never seen a mage do that before."

I ignored the bound woman, and looked at Alec. "Can you move her out of the way? I need some room to work."

He picked up the witch and threw her over his shoulder. The woman let out a shriek.

Quickly, I mumbled the words for a silence spell, then pointed my finger at her. The cries she was making ceased. "That's better."

I'd now done more magic in the last hour than I'd done in years. Most of my magic was limited to detection spells lately and there was something refreshing, almost pleasant about dusting off this part of me.

Alec appeared at my side as I stood in front of the open back door to the car. "You want me to carry them out?"

"Yes please," I said. "Just carefully lay them on the ground."

Alec nodded, then gently lifted each woman out of the car, resting them on the ground.

I set down the jar of fennel powder and checked Dima for a pulse, then I moved to McKenzie. Letting out a sigh of relief I looked up at the muted redhead in the corner of the garage. "It's your lucky day, they're still alive."

15

*M*oonbeam made a gurgling sound as she tried to talk and found that she couldn't. I ignored her and focused on my friends. "Alec, see if you can find something to cut through the webbing. I'm going to get them ready."

It wasn't a difficult spell, but butterflies still filled my insides. Could I still do this kind of healing magic? Taking a deep breath, I recalled the other spells I'd used tonight. They still seemed to work. Maybe casting spells was one of those things you never really forgot. What was that human saying? Like riding a horse?

Shaking out my hands, I focused on clearing my mind. Now wasn't the time to have a crisis or doubt myself.

Kneeling down, I sat back on my heels, so I was in between the spider's victims. The purple color had spread from their tongues and both Dima and McKenzie now had purple lips. Veins of purple spread from their mouths through their cheeks. McKenzie even had a few of the lines on her chin. If the poison got much further, they probably wouldn't make it. It was now or never.

Alec returned with a pair of shears and a box cutter in his hands. "How are these?"

"Fine," I said. "See if you can get through the webbing on Dima. I'll do the spell on McKenzie first. She's further gone."

"Is there anything else I can do?" Alec asked.

"Just stay quiet and don't talk to me until I'm done," I said.

"Got it, boss," he said.

Slowly, I opened the jar of fennel powder and tipped some of it into my cupped hand. "I know this is gross, McKenzie, but it's better than you dying."

I spit into the powder and mixed it with my finger until it formed a paste. Then, I scooped the globs of fennel paste onto my fingers and spread it over her mouth, across her cheeks, and down her chin. The paste would help pull the poison out of her system while I used magic to draw it there.

Wiping the extra fennel paste on my jeans, I leaned over McKenzie's face, my palms hovering above her heart. I closed my eyes and thought about the spell before I said the words. Usually, I was in the habit of saying spells as quietly as possible. It was a survival move, made it so other mages and people who wanted to hurt you didn't know what you were going to do. This time, I couldn't do that. This spell had to be spoken clearly and with conviction. Right to the ears of the gods themselves. Especially in this circumstance. If the gods were real, if they were out there, I could use any help they were willing to give me.

One more time, I repeated the words in my head, making sure they sounded right before I tried them out loud. Hoping I wasn't forgetting anything, I cleared my throat, then spoke as clearly and confidently as I could, "Surge, medici, tollere dolor, et sana vulnus, mundate cor meum."

Something cool started in my toes, a tingling, that rolled through me like a wave, crashing down to my fingertips. The sensation knocked me back and I gasped as I regained my balance. My head felt like it was floating and a lingering taste of something metallic filled my mouth. I reached up to touch my lips, then pulled my hand away. Dots of blood stained my fingers. Using my shirt, I wiped at the blood on the edge of my mouth. I'd forgotten about the higher price of this kind of magic. Being so out of practice made the reaction more intense than it should be.

"Got her free. Oh shit, I wasn't supposed to talk." Alec looked over at me. He had the guilty expression of a child caught breaking the rules. Then his brow furrowed. "You okay, Morgan?"

I wiped my mouth again, figuring I must have missed a spot. "I'm okay, just a reaction to the spell."

"You never said anything about that," he said. "Are you hurt?"

"I'm fine. It just takes a lot out of a mage to do this kind of spell," I said.

"Did it work?" Alec was staring at McKenzie. She was still covered in the fennel goop and didn't look any better than she had been.

"The spell worked, now it's a matter of her body doing the work to rid her of the toxins." I pointed to the paste covering her lower face. "See the purple tint to this? All the poison has to find its way out, then we can wipe off the fennel, and she should wake up."

A violent shuffling sound echoed through the empty garage. I looked up at Dima's body to see her thrashing. Her arms and feet slammed against the cement floor and her body rolled and writhed. She looked like she was having a seizure. This time, there was no time for preparing myself. "Hand me the jar. The jar. Now!"

Alec slammed the fennel powder jar into my waiting hand. I poured a generous amount into my hand and spit several times into it, not wasting any time making the paste.

"Hold her still, Alec," I said.

He straddled her, using his thighs to keep her body from

rolling around and grabbed her arms, pinning them to the ground.

Without hesitation, I turned my whole palm upside down and rubbed the goop all over her mouth, cheeks, and neck. "Keep her still."

One deep breath and a moment to wipe the excess paste on my now filthy jeans, then I stretched out my hands over her heart. "Surge, medici, tollere dolor, et sana vulnus, mundate cor meum."

The words came out easier this time, and again, I was hit with the sensation of something cold, almost like water, rushing through me. Again, it crashed into my fingertips, threatening to knock me off balance. This time, I was prepared and merely swayed before regaining composure.

Warm, wet metallic blood lingered on my tongue and I brought my hands away from Dima to use my shirt to clean myself up. After this, I was in desperate need of a change of clothes.

I hoped the blood wasn't getting to Alec. We'd never had a conversation before about what he could handle seeing. Did being around human blood make him struggle or cause him to want to feed?

Dropping the edge of my ruined tee-shirt, I looked over at him. He wasn't even paying the least bit attention to me. His eyes were glued to Dima, staring at her, waiting for the venom to leave her system.

He'd abandoned the shears nearby, so I picked them up and spun around to face the still webbed McKenzie. The paste on her face was nearly all purple now, and I couldn't see any lines of poison extending beyond her mouth. It wouldn't be long now before she woke up.

Carefully, I tucked one of the blades of the shears under the edge of the sticky web and worked my way through. By the time

I'd cut through, my hands and arms felt like I'd dipped them in a vat of rubber cement. Forget needing a change of clothes, I needed a shower. And these clothes probably needed to be burned.

Rolling her to one side, then the other, I did my best to clear away as much of the web as possible. McKenzie's fingers twitched as I pulled the last bit of webbing away from her.

I leaned over her face, and used my index finger to wipe away a section of the paste from her mouth. Her lips were no longer purple.

Since my clothes were already done for, I tugged on the sleeve, hoping I could tear it off. It did not work like it did in the movies. Instead, I grabbed the sticky shears and managed to cut off both of my sleeves for rags.

Using one of my freed sleeves, I wiped all the paste off of McKenzie's face. Leaning in closer to her face, I narrowed my eyes, trying to see if there was any sign of the purple spider venom. Tension eased as I decided it was all clear.

McKenzie's eyes sprang open and she screamed.

I was on my knees, hovering an inch above her face, and fell back onto my butt, away from her.

She sat up slowly, and started brushing off her clothes. "What happened? Why do I feel like there's a million tiny insects crawling around inside me?"

Alec and I looked at each other, then back at her. Would she want to know that she'd almost been spider food? I wasn't sure I'd want to hear it.

"Please tell me the million blinking eyes was a dream," she said.

"Um," I started, trying to decide which parts to say and which to leave out.

"Hey, what's going on?" Dima's groggy voice came from behind us.

I launched myself toward her, and before I knew it, I was in a group hug, sandwiched between Dima and Alec.

"Okay, okay, I get it, something bad happened," Dima said. "Can you let me breathe now?"

Dima pulled away and wiped the fennel paste off of her mouth, a look of disgust on her face. "Do I even want to know?"

"And can you at least tell us why there's a bound woman in the corner crying?" McKenzie said.

Alec released us, and I let go of Dima. I'd forgotten about Moonbeam in all the chaos.

Ignoring McKenzie's questions, I jumped to standing and walked toward Moonbeam. Sure enough, the witch had tears running down her face.

I scowled at her. "Upset to see that my friends are alive?"

She opened then closed her mouth, still bound by my silence spell.

Wondering how quickly I would regret it, I released her from both spells. She dropped her hands and let out a sob then stuttered a few times, making sounds that weren't quite words.

"What happened?" Dima asked.

I looked behind me to see the rest of the group in a semi-circle around me.

"Are you going to kill me?" Moonbeam asked.

"We're murderers now?" Dima asked. "Wow, I missed a lot."

"No, we're not going to kill you unless you think we should," I said.

Moonbeam licked her lips and swallowed. It was as if she was re-learning how to speak. After what felt like far too long, she finally spoke, "What I told you about the vampires is true. They aren't allowed here, but if you go now, I won't call anyone."

"What was with all the theatrics and the not wanting to help us?" Alec said.

"I'm here on a probationary status. I thought if I could catch a vampire and turn him in, they might grant me permanent residency."

"Permanent residency? What the hell kind of place is this and why would you want to live here?" Alec said.

"Can someone just start at the beginning for me?" McKenzie asked, clearly frustrated.

"You're going to have to wait on that, McKenzie," I said. Then I turned back to Moonbeam. "What is this place? Why are there no cars and why do you have to apply to live here?"

"I told you, it's Nowhere. We're a magical commune. A safe haven for those with magical abilities to live in peace. Without fear of humans or predators like vampires." She nodded at Dima. "They aren't thrilled about Sirens, but with the right reasons, they'd let one in."

Dima growled at the witch, making her back up against the wall.

I put my hand up, signaling Dima to calm down. "How are you here then?"

"Yeah," McKenzie said. "You're practically screaming human."

"I have mage blood in my line. A few generations back, so it's faint. But I'm a gifted witch, everyone says so," Moonbeam was defensive now.

"Whatever," I waved her away. "Moonbeam, you're a terrible person. Trying to lure in someone and prevent them from saving their friends. But you clearly don't need any help to feel miserable. It's obvious you already hate yourself and we've wasted too much time already."

I knelt down and picked up the jar of fennel powder and the lid. There was enough left to do one or two more spells on the bottom. I screwed on the lid. "I'm going to take this with us, just in case. And you, you're going to sit down on the ground and not move until we've been gone for an hour."

"I will not." Moonbeam balled her hands into fists and took a few angry steps toward me.

From behind me, I heard the familiar sounds of a binding spell and before Moonbeam could move any closer, she was once again wrapped in magic tendrils.

McKenzie stood next to me now. "Want me to lock her in place for the next hour?"

I glared at Moonbeam. I'd tried to feel sorry for her, tried to let her learn her lesson and just move on, but she wasn't getting it. She'd stood in my way and nearly cost me the life of my friends. "Better make it two hours."

Letting McKenzie work the spell, I walked over to the car and opened the driver side door. "I'm driving. Everyone else, in the car."

16

"So there really was a giant spider?" Dima asked.

"Yes, it was horrible. Huge, hairy legs, hundreds of eyes," Alec said.

I turned back onto the freeway, happy to be away from the creepy town of Nowhere and made a note to look it up when I got home. It seemed like something that could use a bit of exploration and I wondered if the Mage Order already knew about it.

"...Morgan lit the thing on fire and the next thing we knew, the whole gas station was blazing," Alec continued.

My attention returned to the story of Morgan versus the monster spider at the mention of my name. "I think we've heard it enough times now."

"That's not the best part," Alec said, either not listening to me, or ignoring me. "You should have seen how Morgan handled that crazy witch and her legion of fake hunters. I mean, I thought we were dead. A whole group of vampire hunters closing in on us. But Morgan didn't even flinch." He paused. "Hey, Morgan, did you know they were fake or were you just lucky?"

"I knew," I said. "I don't have a death wish. But, seriously, story time is over. We need a plan. Fast."

"Right," he said.

"We're still headed to the mines, right?" Dima asked. "The plan hasn't changed due to a few hiccups?"

"Yes, we're headed to the mine, but what do we do when we get there?" I asked. "That spider wasn't there on accident. It had to have been sent by someone."

The car was silent as the realization sunk in.

"You think the Dragon-Bloods knew we'd be stopping at that particular gas station?" McKenzie said. "Seems unlikely to me."

"Not if they have a seer," Dima said.

I had been thinking it, but didn't want to say it out loud. If the Dragon-Bloods had a seer, and they knew where we'd be before we went there ourselves, how would we outsmart them?

"You don't think that's a possibility, do you?" McKenzie asked. "There are few seers in the world who can predict with that much accuracy."

I shuddered, recalling the seer I'd encountered as a child. He'd used me as a test subject to see how far he could push his powers, calling me his ladybug. My skin crawled recalling those days.

Pushing the memory away, I focused on the matter at hand. Dr. Byers had left Realm's Gate when he was caught experimenting on children and I hadn't heard of him since. I liked to imagine that he'd been eaten by something terrible.

"The future is always changing," I said. "But there are variations of it. If they have a seer, we have to start choosing the variation that is the last one they'll expect from us."

"Like us working with Tavas?" Alec said.

"Even if we wanted to find him, we don't even know where to start," I said. "And the dragon mages are running out of time."

"It is the last thing anyone would guess you'd do," Dima said.

"Especially if their seer saw you forgo it even after you were told to do it."

"Like I said, how would we even find him?" I asked.

"There's an underground supernatural casino in downtown LA," Alec said.

"You're kidding, right?" I said.

"I have no idea where Tavas hangs out, but it seems like as good a place as any to start," Alec said.

"What makes you think Tavas would be at a casino?" I asked.

Alec shrugged. "I've seen other Fae there. Maybe it's a Fae hangout."

"Aren't Fae illegal?" Dima asked.

"Technically, only dark Fae are illegal," I said, then instantly felt dirty. It was almost like I was defending Tavas, which was the last thing I wanted to do.

"There's all kinds of Fae at this place. You might not want to go around asking them if they are there legally," Alec said. "In fact, maybe you should stay in the car."

"Hey, I can handle myself," Dima said.

"That's clear from the spider web we had to cut off of you," Alec said.

"Enough," McKenzie said. "I know none of you want me here, but it's not a half bad idea."

"We're hours away from there, and the clock is ticking." Seeing Tavas was still not high on my list of priorities, even if the idea was starting to make sense. And I really didn't want to agree with McKenzie.

"It's on the way to the factory," Dima said, waving a large folding map from the back seat.

"Where'd you get that?" I asked.

"Shoved it in my back pocket right before I went down," she said.

If it wasn't out of the way, there wasn't much I could do to argue against at least looking. "Okay, we'll go in and see if he's there. If he's not there, we leave right away. No hanging around to wait for him."

I glanced up at the mirror and looked at Dima and McKenzie in the back seat. "And you two stay in the car."

"Hey, I'm supposed to be here to help keep you safe," McKenzie said.

"Right, spider, remember?" I said.

"That was a fluke," she said. "I can almost guarantee we won't run into a monster like that again."

"Do you even know what that thing was?" I asked.

"No, do you?" McKenzie asked with a defensive tone in her voice.

"No, but we don't know what the long term effects of that will be. We don't know if you've been weakened, or..."

"I get it," McKenzie snapped. "But if we wait in the car, you leave us the keys. At least I can pretend I'm the getaway driver in case the shit hits the fan."

"That's not a half bad idea with the crowd we'll see in there," Alec said.

I looked over at him. "Is it going to be a problem having you in there? How did you leave these people?"

I'd worked for Jimmy long enough to learn that once you joined a criminal organization like his, you didn't leave alive. What had Alec done before he joined Jimmy? Whatever it was, he'd probably been in a similar line of work and he'd managed to impress a very hard to impress ancient vampire.

"I'll be fine," Alec said.

I waited for him to elaborate, but he kept quiet.

We drove for another half-hour or so before I noticed my eyelids getting heavy. Fighting against a yawn, I finally lost, opening my mouth wide.

"You need to sleep," Alec said. "How long has it been?"

I thought back over the whirlwind of the last few days. Everything seemed to blend together. I wasn't even sure what day it was or how long we'd been gone.

The car was quiet as I blinked back the exhaustion. That's when I realized the back seat was silent. "They asleep?"

"Have been for a while," Alec said. "You should be, too."

"It's not like we just go to a hotel," I said. "We've lost too much time already."

"That's the perk of having a vampire on your road trip," he said. "Pull over, I'll drive, you sleep."

Knowing that my driving was going to get dangerous soon, I agreed, and pulled the car into the shoulder. It was around midnight, so the roads were practically empty. I waited as a semi-truck passed, then opened the car door and walked around the back of the car.

Alec held the passenger door open for me. "It's going to be okay, you know that, right?"

"No, I don't know that," I said. "But I want it to be."

"I know," he said. "We're going to find him. And your friend."

I didn't say anything this time, I just nodded and moved around Alec and ducked into the car. Alec closed the door behind me, then a moment later, he was in the driver seat.

"Los Angeles, here we come," he said as he clicked his seat belt in place.

I fastened my own seat belt and locked the door before leaning back in the chair. Closing my eyes, I focused on slowing my breathing. If I was going to sleep, I might as well help it get to me faster.

Trying to shut out everything, I pushed the swirling thoughts from my mind. Visions of Lyla and James tied up or bleeding out kept punctuating my attempts at stillness. Then, it was the blinking eyes of the spider and the sound of its legs clicking across the tile.

I shivered and repositioned myself. For a moment, I found myself recalling my mom's funeral. That was the last place I wanted to go in my head. Things hadn't been the same since she died. I'd been so upset, so sure the Order had let us down, that I skipped town. It was surprisingly easy to get a fake ID and a job in the human world if you can use magic.

I'd worked for a few months in a coffee shop, then moved on to a receptionist job, before finally working as a front desk attendant for the dorms at an art college. I sat there and doodled or surfed the web with the occasional interruption of scanning in a student ID card. It was mind-numbing and boring. Then one day, I got a read off of a student entering the building that I hadn't felt in a while. It was genuine magic. That student, and the unhealthy relationship he brought me, had been the catalyst that drove me back to Realm's Gate.

Frustrated that I'd let myself travel down memory lane, I tried burrowing deeper into the chair and let myself think about James. His smile, his bright blue eyes, that hair. That was a much better mental image to try to fall asleep to.

Suddenly, my memory of James vanished, as if pulled away from me and I was standing alone in the dark. There was an odd glowing quality to my skin when I looked down at my fingertips. I could still see my body, despite the darkness. My heart started pounding. This was the same thing that happened when I connected with James.

Hope rose inside me. He'd said we were connected through the favor, that he could communicate with me. I turned in a slow circle hoping I'd see him alive and well. There was nothing around me in the void. My shoulders sunk as I recalled our last meeting in this place. He said he could connect with me while I was performing magic. I wasn't performing magic. I must have fallen asleep. This was a dream. Or a nightmare.

Cautiously, I took a few steps ahead, wondering if I should

try to make myself wake up, or if I should just lie down and sleep in here. It was the strangest dream for me, though I supposed that after my meeting with James it only made sense that I'd hope to see him again. Why couldn't I dream about him? Why dream about being alone in the darkness? Even my dreams were depressing right now.

"Hello, little dragon," a smooth as silk voice came from behind me.

My insides prickled. I knew that voice. Slowly, I turned around to come face to face with Tavas.

17

"*H*ow are you doing this?" I didn't owe a favor to Tavas. If anything, I owed him a punch in the gut for abandoning me after saying he'd help me, then later turning me in. "And why are you here?"

"You were looking for me, weren't you? I mean, at least that's what I thought I heard." He smiled, but there was something missing from his usual confident appearance.

I realized that he was wearing clothes that were wrinkled and dirty. His jeans were torn at the knee, and not in a fashionable, purposeful way. Green and brown stains covered his clothes. I squinted, then my eyes widened in disbelief as I realized he had twigs and grass or something in his hair.

I took a few steps closer to him and as I neared him, I noticed the scrapes on his chiseled cheekbones. "What happened to you?"

He rolled his eyes. "Just say it. You're happy to see me like this."

Forehead wrinkled, I stared at him. Wasn't I happy to see that he'd been struggling? Shouldn't I be happy that he was hurt and getting some kind of payback for what he did? My stomach twisted. As much as I wanted him to suffer, he was James's friend. And he might be my ticket to finding both James and the missing mages. "You don't even know me, how could you know what I'm thinking?"

"Fine, whatever, you're a saint who doesn't wish harm on anyone, can we move on now?" He glanced behind him, as if expecting someone to join us. Or attack him.

The hair on my arms rose as a sinking feeling settled in the pit of my stomach. Maybe something was after him. Had he brought it here? "What's going on, Tavas?"

"You're the one who called me. It's been rather annoying, honestly. I wouldn't have come, but frankly, I'm tired of ignoring you." He gestured to his chest and legs in a sweeping motion. "And if you can't tell by my wardrobe, I'm in a bit of a conundrum right now."

"What do you mean I called you?" I asked. Sure, the Oracle had told me to find Tavas, but I'd spent the last few days thinking of ways around it. Or trying not to think about Tavas.

"You and your mage friends. That whole spell you did. It opened a connection, one I might add I ignored. But since then, you keep showing up in my head, and I'm rather fond of being alone in my own head," he said. "By the way, impressive job of taking down the spider."

"You saw that?" My voice came out high-pitched and irritated. "What else have you seen? Are you watching me?"

Tavas let out a frustrated sigh, and looked behind him again. "Look, little dragon, I don't have time for this. Just tell me why you want to find me and get out of my head."

"First," I said. "I'm not in your head. And I honestly didn't want to find you, but the Oracle said I had to find you."

Tavas scoffed. "That old fraud, you believed him? Did he pull out his Tarot deck and read you a fortune?"

I knew Tavas wasn't really here, but even in whatever form

this was, he was irritating. I rubbed my forehead, wondering how I was going to work with this Fae without wanting to kill him.

"Look, I've got to go, please stop trying to talk to me," Tavas said, turning away from me.

"Wait!" I ran up to him and grabbed hold of his upper arm.

Tavas turned and looked at me in disgust. "Seriously, I get it, I'm attractive. But I'm afraid it just isn't going to work."

"Get over yourself, you spoiled brat," I said. "James is in trouble. And I don't know who else can help."

"I'm sorry, love, but I have my own problems right now," Tavas said.

"You owe me," I said.

"I don't owe you shit." He pulled his arm from my grasp.

"Then you owe James. You know he saved us both." I watched as a flicker of conflict flashed in his green eyes. "I have a feeling you owe him for a lot more than saving us in that alleyway."

Tavas shook his head. "Fine, but you're going to have to help me first."

"We don't have time for that," I said. "Just tell me where you are and we'll pick you up."

"I'm in Cleveland," he took a few steps away from me. "But if you're not here soon, I won't be able to help you because I'll be dead."

"Cleveland? How the..." my words trailed off as Tavas vanished from sight.

Suddenly, a vision of a warehouse filled my mind. It was so real, like I was standing there in person. I could smell the factory smoke and feel the wind blowing past me. This wasn't a normal vision, this was a location. He was downloading it to my subconscious. Tavas expected me to teleport.

I woke with a start, feeling fully awake, and fully pissed off.

Leave it to that Fae to be on the other side of the continent, needing help, when we needed him.

"Bad dream?" Alec asked.

"How do you feel about Cleveland?" I asked.

"What's in Cleveland?" he said.

"Tavas," I said.

"How do you know that?" Alec said.

"He found me in my dreams." The words sounded ridiculous as I said them, but I knew what I saw. It was real. "And he's in trouble. We're going to have to get there fast."

"We're probably not far from the airport," Alec said.

I shook my head. "No time for airports."

"Driving will take forever. You can't think that's faster."

"No, not driving." I looked behind me at the sleeping forms of my friends. "We're going to have to wake them. I'll need more magic than what I have."

"There's a magical way to get to Cleveland?" Alec said.

"Yep, and they're not going to be happy about it." Dread filled me as I considered how I was going to ask McKenzie and Dima to share their magic with me so we could teleport. Neither of them had been in the car with James when I helped him teleport. And to be honest, I wasn't sure how much of the magic had come from me, and how much had come from him. I wasn't even sure I'd be able to duplicate it again.

What I did know was that we were running out of time. And for some reason, we needed Tavas. Who, of course, happened to be nowhere near where we needed him. I hardly knew Tavas, but I should have expected that finding him wouldn't be convenient for us. And I should have known that it would come with strings. Whatever trouble he was in, we were going to have to walk right into it and bail him out. Why couldn't things just be normal in my life?

"Don't even say it," McKenzie said.

I pursed my lips. For someone who had been raised in the human world, she seemed quick to pick up on where I was going with this. Part of me was hoping that being the only mage in the car would be an advantage to convincing my friends.

"What are you thinking of doing?" Dima asked. "And why do I suddenly feel like I might agree with McKenzie for once?"

"Look, it might not be as dangerous as you think," I said.

"Can someone please explain what the hell you're talking about here?" Alec asked.

"Say it, Morgan. Just say the word." McKenzie made it sounds like a challenge, which fired me up a bit. She didn't know me. She didn't know what I was capable of. I'd already saved her life once and she didn't even have to be here. Nobody wanted her here.

"Teleportation, and before you get judgy, McKenzie, I've done it before. And I'm not dead."

"That doesn't mean anything," she said. "The history books are full of people who successfully teleported multiple times. It's the one time that it's not successful that kills you."

"Even I know how dangerous that is," Dima said. "Isn't there another way?"

"Wait, you can teleport?" Alec asked. "Why am I driving? Let's just get this over with and go save your friends."

"Because it's dangerous, you dumbass," McKenzie said.

"Hey, we can leave you right here if you don't want to go," I said to McKenzie. "In fact, anyone who is afraid can stay here. There's no reason to risk us all."

"Is it seriously that big of a deal?" Alec asked. "I mean, I've seen you do some really amazing stuff over the last few days." He glanced over at me and smiled. "If she says she can do it, I believe her."

"Well, shit, make me look like the bad friend," Dima said.

"You're not a bad friend if you don't go," I said. "I get it, it's not something we're used to doing, and it's got a shaky outcome sometimes."

"When did you teleport?" McKenzie's words were quieter this time, almost reverent. Was it possible she believed me? That she was finally seeing that I was able to take care of myself?

"A couple of days ago, with James," I said.

"And James is?" McKenzie asked.

The car was silent. Neither of my friends spoke up. We hadn't told the Mage Order about James. Nobody knew about him yet. The last thing I wanted was power-hungry mages or who knew who else hunting down one of the only dragon shifters in our realm. "He's a friend of ours who lived outside of Realm's Gate."

"Did the Dragon-Bloods get him, too?" she asked.

I let out a small breath of relief. McKenzie assumed he was a mage, like me. "Yes, they got him too."

"I've never seen anyone teleport," McKenzie said. "Can you take us with you? How does that work?"

"Are you saying you'll go?" I was surprised that she was handling this so well. I knew she had orders to go with us, so I expected that she'd tag along unless the others refused to go with me. What I didn't expect was so little conversation around talking me out of it.

"Well, you said you need this Tavas, right? It's the only way?"

"Yes, as much as I hate to admit it, we need him." I tried to hide the disgust in my voice.

"How do we get there, then?" Dima asked this time. "Do you need us to hold hands or something?"

"Not exactly," I said. "Actually, I can teleport us in the car. But I'm going to need to borrow magic from all of you."

18

"*W*hat do you mean by *borrowing magic*?" McKenzie sounded skeptical, the tone I expected her to use from the very beginning.

"Like you did to get into James's house?" Alec asked.

"Yes," I said, then turned to face the women in the back seat. "You can share your magic with me to make mine stronger, like a group mage spell."

"Oh," McKenzie said. "You're talking about when they do the divination table or reinforce the wards."

"Exactly," I said. "And Dima, you can share yours, too. I was able to channel some of Alec's so I think you'll be able to help."

"I don't have magic," Dima said.

"Yes, you do," Alec said. "She found some in me, I'm guessing you have lots more. Look what you made me do the first night we met."

"There's a story in that, I'm sure," McKenzie said.

"Later," I said. "Alec, pull over the car."

The blinker sounded as Alec pulled the car into the shoulder, vibrating over the cut marks on the freeway before slowing to a stop.

"I hate sharing magic. I've only done it once and it was awful," McKenzie said, breaking the heavy silence in the air.

"I know," I said. It was an odd thing for a mage to share magic. Our magic was what made us who we were, it was part of us. When it was taken or given, it left you feeling weak and uncomfortable.

The few times I'd shared magic, I'd spent an hour recovering with a sense of emptiness that I couldn't shake. That was something I appreciated about being away from the mage community. Aside from the last few days, nobody had expected me to do group spells. And I'd been on the receiving end, which sent a rush of power through me. That wasn't a bad thing. I was asking a lot of McKenzie. More so than the others, who likely didn't notice their magic in the same way.

"If there was another way," I began, but didn't finish the statement.

"Let's just get this over with," McKenzie said.

I nodded at McKenzie. She knew that moving forward, we'd share a bond that only mages knew. I might even have to start being nice to her.

Taking a deep breath, I looked at the faces of all the people in the car with me. They all looked nervous, but determined. It was probably the best I would get from them. "I'm going to need focus from everyone to make this work."

My lips moved as I practiced the spell silently to myself. Even though I'd successfully done this before, my stomach churned as nervous butterflies flew circles in my midsection. I knew I needed to maintain a sense of confidence. These people were counting on me. I had to be a leader. "Alright, everyone, first I'm going to ask you to channel your magic and I'm going to pull from it. You might feel something different, I need you to let it happen, support it even. Once I have enough, I'm going to cast the spell."

"Wait, do you know the exact location?" McKenzie asked.

"Yes," I said. "Tavas was very specific in his instructions, don't worry."

She took a deep breath and nodded, clearly worried.

"Please do not think of any places, only think of sending me your magic. Only think of reinforcing the spell. Keep your minds focused on sharing your magic, on supporting me while I cast this, nothing else. Especially not other locations," I said.

"Great, now all I can think of is the Margarita bar in TJ," Dima said.

"Do not think about that," I said.

"I won't. Don't worry, I got this." She smiled. "But if we survive all of this, we're getting margaritas when we're done."

"Deal," I said.

"If you two are done, can we just get this over with?" McKenzie said.

"She's right. Tavas said he needed help, we shouldn't wait any longer," Alec said.

I nodded. "Right, here goes." Closing my eyes, I concentrated on the magic inside me. The magic that was embedded deep down, the place I hadn't used in years and somehow ended up having to access all too often lately. The swirling tingle of magic filled my insides, warm and welcome like an old friend.

Stretching my fingers out, I offered a hand to Dima and McKenzie in the back. McKenzie took hold without waiting for directions. Dima followed suit.

Extending my other hand to Alec, I nodded for him to take it. Silently, he took hold and almost instantly, I felt a charge roll through me. The hair on my arms stood on end as my friends focused on sending me their magic. I whispered an amplification spell and the rush that filled me made me gasp.

Alec's brow furrowed in concern, but he remained quiet, focused on the task at hand.

I nodded to the women in the back and to Alec before taking a deep breath and closing my eyes. It was now or never. Time to teleport on my own. Using the information that Tavas gave me, I focused on the warehouse he'd shown me. The exact location was vital, but a clear mental image could be used if it had enough power behind it. And the vision that Tavas had shared with me seemed to be embedded with magic, like a line of code on a computer, it clicked into place, sending my brain whirring as I murmured the words.

Something tugged in the pit of my stomach, throwing me back so hard that my hand was pulled from my friends, and I landed with a thud against the glove compartment.

My head was spinning and a sudden urge to vomit rose up so fast that without thinking, I pulled open the car door and let it out.

As I wiped my mouth with the back of my hand, I realized that I'd just thrown up on someone's shoes. A pair of black leather designer men's shoes were now ruined thanks to me. They were large shoes, and my hands were shaking as I wondered how big the owner of those shoes was.

Still feeling drained from using so much magic, I swayed as I looked up to see the owner of the shoes. For a fraction of a second, I hoped it was Tavas. But as soon as my eyes traveled up the silk suit pants, to the crisp, white shirt, I knew I wasn't going to be that lucky. My eyes traveled up to the chest, exposed a bit by the open buttons at the neck. Then, I reached the beautiful, chiseled face, green eyes, and pale blonde hair of a very hand-some man.

While I wasn't looking at Tavas, the slight point to the ears of this newcomer let me know I was face-to-face with another Fae. The blonde Fae lifted an eyebrow and pursed his lips. He did not look happy with me.

I shook my head for a moment, trying to regain a sense of reality. "I'm so sorry."

His upper lip curled and his nose crinkled as he looked down at his shoes, then he looked back at me. "I wish I could say this was the first time a woman did that to my shoes."

Now it was my turn to lift my eyebrows in surprise. "Really? That's happened before?"

"Do you know this guy?" McKenzie said from the back seat.

"Oh," I was so mortified by the fact that I'd thrown up on a stranger's shoes that I forgot the whole reason we were here. "Yeah, no. I have no idea who this is."

"Luka," the Fae said, then he pressed himself against me and peered into the back seat. "Hello."

I shifted in my seat and moved myself as far away from him as I could. Luka backed up so he was standing in front of the door again. "You four want to tell my why you teleported right into the location for the annual Fae Summit?"

"Fae Summit?" Dima said. "Seriously, Morgan?"

I ignored Dima's comments and smiled at Luka. "We thought a friend was in trouble, so we came at their request." I didn't see any reason to lie to him, so I kept it as simple as possible.

Luka shrugged. "Well, unless you're friends with that low-life, Tavas, you have nothing to be worried about."

My shoulders sunk.

"You're friends with Tavas?" Luka asked, seeming genuinely surprised.

"I wouldn't say we're exactly friends," I said. "But, yes, we're here for Tavas."

"I really wish you wouldn't have said that," Luka said. "If it had been anyone else, I could have let you leave. Now, I'm going to have to take you in."

"Alec, gun it," McKenzie called.

"I don't think that's a good idea," Alec said.

I looked over at him. Alec's gaze was locked ahead of him. Following his stare, my mouth dropped open and a cold chill ran through me. There were a dozen or so Fae standing in front of our car.

"Like I said," Luka said. "I'm going to have to take you in."

hatever it was that Luka used to tie my wrists together in front of me, it was strong. I tried pulling my arms apart and the ties didn't budge. We'd all grown up with stories about the Fae and we'd all been warned about how dangerous they were. But it never seemed to matter. They weren't allowed in our realm, or so I thought, which meant I never expected to run into any. I didn't even know if the things I'd learned about them were true. Was iron really their only weakness?

"Can you tell us what's going on?" I said. "We didn't mean any harm."

"That's not my call," Luka said as he led me into a small building next to the warehouse.

As I crossed the threshold, I was greeted by buzzing florescent lights and the smell of stale coffee. Thin, brown carpet covered the floor and you could see a path worn into it from the traffic patterns in the room. A few cubicles were set up with desks and computers and a table with a burgundy couch took up a corner. I was guessing it was a waiting area of some kind.

Luka took his hand off of me for the first time since tying my wrists, then he lifted his chin toward the couch. "Have a seat. The Magistrate will be with you shortly. She'll decide what we do with you."

Knowing there was no way we could fight off the whole group of Fae, I swallowed, then walked to the couch. I sat down in the middle and the springs gave way as I sunk into the worn down cushion.

Without a word, Dima, Alec, and McKenzie sat down on either side of me, making me sink further into the couch from the additional weight.

"We'll be outside," Luka said.

I watched as Luka and the other Fae left through the door they'd taken us in. As soon as it closed, I started looking around the room, hoping to find another exit.

"This was a bad idea," Dima said. "Why are there so many Fae here? I thought they were banned from our realm."

"We should have let Tavas rot," Alec said.

"It was probably a trap the whole time, how did we not see this?" McKenzie whispered.

"Enough," I said. "No arguing, we can't do anything to change this. Right now, we have to work together to get out of here."

"Can't you two just magic us out?" Alec asked.

"Probably," McKenzie said. "If we hadn't just used everything we had to teleport here."

"I can't even charm my way out of anything right now," Dima said. "Plus, I don't know if it would work on the Fae anyway."

"Maybe diplomacy is our best bet?" I suggested. "Maybe this Magistrate will understand. I mean, most of us were taught to revere the Oracle, maybe she'll let us borrow Tavas and go."

"We're taught that here, what are they taught in Faerie?" Dima asked.

Her words rang true and I leaned back against the couch. What was I going to do? We needed to save James; we needed to save Lyla and the other dragon mages. We shouldn't even be here.

Tugging at the cord on my wrist again, I wondered if we could make a run for it. I lifted my wrists up to Alec, who was sitting next to me. "Can you break through these?"

He lifted his bound hands and worked his fingers into the binding. They didn't give. "I don't know what this is, but I can't break through it."

The sound of the door creaking open rang through the room and I dropped my hands.

A Fae woman with long silver hair, wearing a powder-blue suit stepped across the threshold. "You won't be able to break the bindings. It's Fae magic. Too powerful for anything you could cast in this realm."

I glared at her.

She walked with grace, her tall, slender form nearly floating over the threadbare carpet. Pausing in front of the couch, she clasped her hands in front of her and glanced from side to side, as if taking inventory of the four of us on the couch.

"What do you want with us?" I asked.

"*We*, what do *we* want?" she smirked. "You're the ones who teleported into a very important, very secret meeting. We had months of security and scouting to find a place that we could be free from prying eyes. We have wards around the entire complex. Wards that should have prevented anyone from penetrating. You should have been denied entry. You are the invaders here."

"We're not invaders, you're not even allowed to be in this realm," McKenzie said.

"McKenzie," I snapped. "Not now."

The Fae, who I had to assume was the Magistrate, narrowed her eyes and stared at McKenzie. "You might want to hold your tongue before I start sharing your secrets."

McKenzie's face drained of color and she looked down at her hands. I wondered what she was hiding that made her quiet down so quickly. After everything I've been through in the last week, I should have realized that everyone had secrets. Nobody in this life was without their own demons.

"Please, Magistrate," I said. "We didn't mean any harm. We are trying to save our friends and the Oracle said we needed Tavas."

Her forehead wrinkled as she stared at me. She seemed to be considering my words. "What do you need with Tavas?"

"I told you, the Oracle said we needed his help. I don't know any more than that."

"And trust us, if there was a way to avoid his help, we wouldn't be here," Alec added.

The Magistrate laughed, an honest-to-god throw-your-head-back laugh. It was startling. While she was an imposing figure, easily six feet tall, some of my fear broke down as she wiped away a tear on her cheek.

"Look, if you don't want us to take Tavas, that's fine. But we really need to save our friends," I said.

"But I thought you said you have to have him?" she asked.

I blew out a sigh of frustration. "Right, but we're on a deadline here and if we can't have his help, we have to find a different way."

A gentle knock sounded on the door and the Magistrate turned toward the sound. "Enter."

One of the Fae who had escorted us here stepped into the threshold. "It's ready, would you like us to hold?"

The Magistrate looked back at me. "How close are you and my Tavas?"

Startled at her use of the possessive term, my, I flinched before regaining my train of thought. This seemed like a test of some sort and I had no idea how I was supposed to answer. Finally, I settled on the truth. "We're not. He's a friend of a friend. The only reason we're looking for him is because of the Oracle."

She stared blankly at me for a moment, then pressed her lips into a thin line. "Very well, you may challenge for his life. Or you may take your leave."

The Fae holding open the door came forward and stopped in front of me, then waved his hand over my bound wrists. The ties fell to the ground.

I rubbed the place on my wrists where the binding had been even though they didn't hurt. It was nice to be able to move freely again. "What does that mean? How can I challenge?"

The Magistrate turned away from us and walked toward the door, slowly, as if she expected us to follow.

"What kind of challenge?" Alec asked.

Pausing in her step, the Magistrate turned to face us. "He's been sentenced to death. If you'd like to see him alive, I suggest you hurry."

"Of course, he has," I said, irritated. I stood up and shook my head. Of course I'd have to save Tavas from something like this. He seemed the type who pushed his limits and whatever he had done had caught up to him.

Alec grabbed hold of my upper arm, his bindings now free. "Maybe we should just go. We don't owe anything to Tavas."

The Magistrate smiled. "You really do know him, don't you?"

"What did he do?" Dima asked, breaking the silence she'd held since we got here.

"That's our business," the male Fae said, pulling his hands into fists.

Whatever it was, we'd clearly touched a nerve.

The Magistrate lifted her hand, halting the other Fae's movements. "It's fine, Samuel." She turned to me. "Tavas has a great many crimes to atone for. He's been on the run for a while. Most recently, in Realm's Gate."

I stiffened at the mention of my home city. Was she referencing Jimmy or the dragon or was there more I didn't know? I felt that at this point, it probably didn't hurt to say something in Tavas's defense. "The Oracle says he didn't kill Jimmy."

"That's what he said." The Magistrate didn't look convinced.

"If you aren't going to help us, why haven't you just killed us already?" Alec asked.

"Alec!" McKenzie said. "Stop talking."

"We have an alliance with the dragons," the Magistrate said, nodding to me. "So to not anger the mother, we'll give you a chance. If you fail, you'll both die."

"Seriously, Morgan, we should go. Tavas isn't worth it," Dima said.

Part of me was on Dima's side. Part of me wanted to run. But the Oracle said we needed him. And it was starting to look like Tavas might not have betrayed me the way I thought he had. Why couldn't things just be what they seemed? These were the days I wondered if being human was easier. There wasn't as much complication when you didn't know about the Fae, or dragons, or shifters, or any of this.

"Morgan, do you think it's worth it?" Alec asked quietly. "Can we save them without him?"

That was the question, wasn't it? Swallowing hard, I straightened, trying to make myself look braver than I felt. We'd already tried to find the missing mages on our own and so far, we'd been almost eaten by a giant spider and threatened by a witch. We didn't have time for more threats like that. We didn't even have time for this. But I had a feeling that if we didn't save Tavas, we weren't going to make it to the mages in time. I wasn't sure what the Dragon-Bloods had in mind, but whatever it was, it was bad enough to keep James, an elite dragon, in hiding from them. Whatever they had planned, I had to try to stop it. "What do I have to do for this challenge?"

20

We followed the Magistrate out of the small building to find the dozen Fae who had brought us here waiting for us. They stood with their arms crossed and their eyes locked on me. Each man in the group was wearing a black suit. The only thing that made them not look like agents from some spy movie was the lack of sunglasses and the sharp, Fae features.

None of these men would pass for human to anyone who had knowledge of the magical world. They were far too beautiful, and most of them were probably nearing seven feet. I didn't often feel short at five-six, but today, I felt like a child.

The Fae guards bowed their heads and lowered their eyes as the magistrate walked through them. Luka stood at the end of the group, the only one of the men who wore his shirt open. I wondered if his status was different than the rest of the gathered Fae. He extended his arm for the magistrate. He bowed. "Your highness."

My brow furrowed. "Your highness?"

The woman I thought was the Magistrate turned and

glanced at me. "You may call me Meryl, I've never been big on titles, but yes, I'm the Queen of the Fae."

A million questions raced though my mind. What was the Fae Queen doing in the human realm? What was she doing at a Fae Summit? What the hell was this summit? It had to be bigger than I thought since the queen was here. She was risking a lot to be here. But then again, as Tavas said, the Fae were never technically banned from our realm, only the Dark Fae. And she was smart, they weren't meeting in a magical city like Realm's Gate or one of the human cities with a large magical population. Cleveland had to be one of the least magical cities in the United States. That was probably why they chose it.

As my mind raced, I realized I was silently following the queen and her entourage. My friends were behind me and I wondered what they were thinking since none of them were speaking. Were they asking the same questions I was?

The group paused in front of a weather-beaten gray warehouse. The paint on the bottom of the building was peeling and rust was eating away at the exposed metal areas along the ground.

Luka dropped hold of the queen's hand and knocked on the massive door at the center of the wall. He paused, then knocked again, falling into a pattern of knocks and silences.

Vibrations under my feet raced up my legs, sending a rush of magic through me, catching me off guard. I stumbled back, then caught my balance. Every inch of my skin tingled. Whatever Luka was doing wasn't just knocking, he was using magic and it was strong. The whole space seemed to hum with magic, as if he'd flipped a switch that had been suppressing something.

"What's happening?" McKenzie whispered. For the first time on the journey, she sounded scared. Her tough exterior couldn't hold up to this.

"I think they just summoned something," I said. It was the

only explanation I could think of for the magic that was sweeping through the space. There was a shift, as if we were no longer in the same world that we had been.

The Fae ignored our unease as they stared straight ahead, waiting. With a rattle, the massive metal door slid open and magic rushed out like a wave, washing over all of us. It wasn't unlike the feeling of when a ghost passes through you. Like ice water traveling through your very soul, then it was gone.

My heart raced as I blinked against the bright light of the interior of the warehouse. Once my eyes adjusted, I gasped at the sight in front of me. I expected a dingy warehouse. I didn't expect to be looking at a jungle. But that's what I saw in front of me. Thick trees, hanging vines, the sound of birdsong came from the distance and the fresh, clean scent of rain mixed with exotic flowers filled my nostrils. "What is this?"

"It's your challenge," Queen Meryl said. "We opened a portal to Faerie inside this warehouse. Tavas is in there. He's hurt and bleeding, which will draw the predators. If you can find him before they do, you can have him."

Alec moved up next to me. "We can do this."

"You misunderstand," Queen Meryl said. "She's the challenger, that means she goes in alone."

"You can't expect a mage to handle the Fae realm alone! We don't even know if her magic will work in there," Dima said.

"Plus, she used most of her magic to get us here, it's not fair," McKenzie added.

"There was nothing fair about Tavas's crimes. He's getting a second chance he shouldn't be getting." Queen Meryl looked at me. "The choice is yours, either you go in alone and you find him, or you leave now."

"What happens if I don't find him?" I asked.

"And how will she get back out of there?" Dima asked.

Queen Meryl took my hand and turned it so it was palm up.

She dropped something silvery into my open palm. "You can only use this once. It will get you and whomever you are touching back to this place. If Tavas isn't worth it, you can return."

I looked down at my hand and stared at a circular pendant on a silver chain, then nodded at the queen. "Thank you."

"You sure about this?" Dima asked.

I clasped the silver chain around my neck and turned around to see my friends. "I have to try."

Before I could let anyone talk me out of it, I stepped across the threshold into the warehouse. Humidity dampened the air and my clothes stuck to my skin. I knew my normally wavy hair would be working its way into a lion's mane of frizz and wished I had a hair tie to pull it back. Tucking my hair behind my ears, I took a few cautious steps. My feet sunk down into soft earth and I wondered how far this space went. Was this a portal to the entire Fae realm or was this just a piece of it here? Fae magic was so unfamiliar to me that neither would be a surprise.

I turned around to ask the queen, but all I saw were more trees. Slowly, I moved in a circle, wondering if I had turned the wrong direction from the door. But the door was gone. I was standing in the middle of a humid jungle, full of whatever kind of predators they had in Faerie, searching for a wounded Fae that I didn't even like.

With a sigh, I looked up for anything I could use to find my way so I could at least travel in the same direction. The canopy of tress ahead was so dense, I couldn't even tell if it was day or night. It had been dark in Cleveland, but there was enough light in here to see around me. Did that mean it was daytime in Faerie or was there a glow to this forest that didn't exist on earth?

Either way, I was stuck in the middle of a darkened forest with no help to find an injured Fae that I wasn't sure I wanted to find. The only thing I had going for me was the fact that I had a necklace that could get me back to Cleveland. Awesome.

I found myself thinking of Hansel and Gretel, lost in the woods, leaving a trail of breadcrumbs. Wishing I had something to use as a marker. I shoved my hands into the pockets of my jeans. All I found was a quarter, which was of zero use to me.

There wasn't anything I could do, so I started to walk. Stepping over vines and broken tree branches, I made my way deeper into the jungle. My breathing was already heavy, the air seemed thicker here than it was at home. Though my lack of physical exercise probably contributed to my panting.

Part of me just wanted to call out to Tavas, but I knew enough from movies to know that it probably wasn't a good idea to alert potential bad guys to where you were. Meryl had never specified what kind of predators I was up against and I'd spent enough time with Tavas to know that the Fae were not always forthcoming in their words with you. For all I knew, there was a group of Fae on a hunting party out there searching for Tavas and he was the prey.

The thought sent a shiver through me. It was all too gruesome, but the stories of the Fae were the stuff of nightmares. I tried to tell myself that the stories I grew up on were about the Dark Fae, and these were not Dark Fae. So, maybe what I knew was wrong. But then, what kind of people let someone who is bleeding get killed by animals? What did you have to do to earn that kind of punishment? And what kind of animals are we talking about anyway? Was it something like a lion or a bear, or were there worse beasties in the Fae Realm? My stomach twisted into knots as my imagination ran wild. I pictured creatures with horns, and claws, and snouts that stood twice my height.

Nearby, I heard a crack and nearly jumped out of my skin. Looking toward the source, I caught a glimpse of a small animal as it scurried across the branches, shaking the leaves. It almost sounded like rain. I looked up to try to identify the creature. If it looked like something I was familiar with, maybe that would help me calm down.

As I stared up into the trees, I heard the rain-like sound of the branches intensify. Suddenly, a whole swarm of tiny, brown squirrel-like creatures raced over the branches, leaping from tree to tree. I covered my head with my hands as they flew over me, chattering and screeching as they did.

My heart raced as the jungle filled with the sounds of a swarm of these little beasts. Then, everything grew quiet. No more creatures, no more movement in the trees. Not even wind.

Behind me, I heard a low growl.

21

_H_eart thundering in my chest, whole body tense, I slowly turned around. My face twitched as I fought against screaming.

Its upper lip curled back as it growled, and I could see the rows of sharp teeth. Drool dripped from its long curved fangs. The eyes were slitted like a cat's, and it had the ears and spots of a cat. Even on all fours, the teeth were level with my face. If it weren't for the sheer size of the creature, I would have called it a leopard. Well, that and the wings.

As if it knew I was thinking of them, the beast opened its wings, showing the impressive wingspan. Then, it threw its head back and let out a roar, sending spit all over my face and making my ears ring.

I wiped off my face with my shoulder as best I could without taking my eyes off of the creature. What was it you were supposed to do if you ran into a wild animal? I vaguely recalled something about bears, but I had no idea what it was. And this was not a bear. It could probably eat a bear.

"Nice kitty," I said, taking a few steps backward. "Nice kitty. I'm not going to hurt you."

The creature resumed its growling and with heavy steps, it moved closer to me. I looked around, wondering if there was anything I could use as a weapon. I'd defeated a giant spider with pure luck. If there hadn't been lighter fluid in reach, there was no way I would have survived. This time, all I had was trees and whatever magic was able to be accessed right now.

My go to was fire, but even if it took in the damp jungle, I was risking staring a fire I couldn't control. One that could potentially hurt the person I was searching for. Figuring the biggest beastie in the woods had found me, I decided silence was no longer my only option. "Tavas?" I tested the word out, afraid to shout and startle the creature.

It advanced again, moving closer to me. I continued stepping backward. I was running out of options. "Tavas!"

My words echoed through the trees, apparently startling a flock of birds who took to flight in a blue cloud, squawking and flapping into the air.

The giant leopard thing turned away from me, shifting its weight toward the birds.

This was my chance. Not wasting a moment, I turned and ran.

Behind me the sound of a roar pierced the air and I picked up the pace, leaping over a fallen log and batting leaves away from my face. There was no time to look back, I had to get away from that monster.

A stabbing pain dug into my side but I tried to power through. I pressed my hand against the pain and focused on my breathing. It didn't ease up. Feeling defeated, I slowed to a walk and risked a peek behind me.

My heart hammered against my ribs so hard it felt like it wanted to break out. Stopping, I looked all around me. There was no sign of the leopard creature. Blowing out a breath, I pushed my hair off of my sweaty forehead.

What the hell was I doing here? How was I going to find Tavas in this mess? Why did I even think I could do this?

Still gripping my side, I kept moving, wondering if it even mattered. The chances of me finding him here were miniscule. Especially if he was hurt and hiding. He could be buried under a pile of leaves right behind me for all I knew.

This wasn't going to work. I wasn't going to find him by wandering around. At this rate, I was more likely to get eaten before I ever found him. For a moment, I considered using the necklace to go back. But we knew there was someone watching us who could predict our plans. If we went straight into the mines to get the mages, they'd be waiting for us. We wouldn't stand a chance. If I could find Tavas, we might have a hope of helping these people and stopping whatever craziness the Dragon-Bloods had in mind.

I needed to stop and think. Running in head first wasn't helping anything. My magic was still weak from teleporting, but there had to be a spell I could use. That's when I remembered how I got here in the first place. Tavas had come to me in a dream. He said he was watching me. Ignoring the crawling, violated feeling that spread through me, I starting pacing in a small circle. If he could see me, could I see him? Was there a way I could duplicate that? A way that I could reach out to him and find out where he was in all these trees?

There had to be a way to use the connection that I'd opened with Tavas to find him. But how do I make it work? I took a few steps, checking my surroundings.

I'd avoided learning any magic that had to do with mind control. After being abused by someone I trusted, I distanced myself from anyone who used magic to make others do what they wanted. Which meant any magic that required me to get into someone's head or let them in mine was something I had little to no experience doing.

Any magic that involved connecting with another person was going to require all of my concentration. It was not my forte by choice, and from what I remembered, if you were in someone else's head, you saw what they saw, leaving you vulnerable. If I was going to do this, I needed to make sure the leopard thing wasn't going to come back and have me for lunch.

Ahead, I saw a tree that had some lower hanging branches. It was possible I could climb up and find a way to wedge myself in the branches. It wasn't a great plan, but right now, it was all I had.

Climbing trees was harder than it seemed in the movies. Gripping the branch above me, I held on, but lost my grip before I could pull myself up. What did I expect? I wasn't an athlete and I had never climbed a tree before in my life.

I looked around again, hoping to find something that looked like it would hide me while I tried to connect with Tavas. The forest wasn't providing me any good options and as I stared around, I noticed that it seemed darker than it had been. How long have I been here? Probably too long already.

Shit. I slid down the tree trunk, setting on the ground at its base. There wasn't any more time. I had to try this and find Tavas. If the leopard or any other monster wanted to eat me, it was going to have at least a few minutes of an easy target. And at this point, I wasn't sure I had enough energy to outrun anything again.

I shook out my hands and took a deep breath. While I hadn't spent time practicing these spells, I'd at least read about them. We still had to take the tests on the spells in school, even if we didn't try them. I recalled the theory behind them, you had to build a connection in the spirit realm, the place that lingered between our world and the afterlife. It was probably the blackness that I'd entered when I spoke with James and when I had spoken with Tavas.

Thinking back to those meetings, I remembered how solid I had felt, how I could touch them while we spoke. It wasn't as intangible as I thought it was. Closing my eyes, I thought back to that place. My breathing was even, and I managed to shut out the noises around me, a sense of calm hung over me. I waited.

Nothing happened.

Tavas? I imagined seeing him and called to him in my head. Nothing.

After what I guessed was several minutes, I opened my eyes. Whatever I was doing, it wasn't working. The forest was definitely getting darker. There was no way I was staying here after dark. It was now or never.

Unsure if it would work, I closed my eyes again. And this time, I spoke the words for the seeking spell. The same spell I had cast in the divination room with the whole group of mages. I knew I didn't have the strength to make this happen on my own, but I had to try.

Cold spread through me and the darkness of the back of my eyelids was replaced by the darkness of what I now knew was the spirit realm. Hope fluttered in my chest. "Tavas?"

I walked around the dark space, my footsteps silent in the blackness. "Tavas? Are you here? I'm trying to find you. I need to know where you are."

"Morgan?" Tavas appeared in front of me, lying on the ground, a hand over a gaping wound on his side. His white button up shirt was soaked with blood.

I ran to him, dropping to my knees by his side. I reached out to his hand. Even though I didn't like Tavas, I could almost feel the pain he was feeling. Every part of me wanted to help him, it was like my insides were screaming but the sound wouldn't leave. "Where are you? How can I find you?"

"Open your eyes, Morgan," Tavas said.

"No, I'm not leaving you here," I said.

Tavas smiled. "Just listen to me for once."

Jaw set in determination, I narrowed my eyes at him. "Are you really prepared to die instead of helping me?"

"Open your damn eyes," Tavas said again.

With a start, I opened my eyes to find that I was no longer leaning against the same tree. Instead, I was kneeling down in front of Tavas, and he was unconscious.

22

*C*radling Tavas in my arms, I grabbed hold of the charm on the necklace. "Get me the hell out of here."

As if I were Dorothy, the world around me began to fade. For some reason, I held my breath and was still holding it when I materialized on the asphalt in front of the warehouse.

Still gripping Tavas, I looked around and saw Dima, McKenzie, and Alec sitting on a cement parking block nearby. The three of them ran toward me.

"Is he alive?" Dima asked.

"That's a lot of blood," Alec said, taking a step back.

"Can you help him?" I asked Alec. "I know it's been a while since you've eaten, but can you give him some blood? He's been hurt badly and I'm not sure what else to do."

"Will it work on a Fae?" Everyone knew that vampire blood had healing properties, but it didn't work the same for every creature. It was most effective on humans and sirens. Less so on shifters and mages. The theory was that the more magic you had, the less effective it was. And the Fae were known for their magic.

"I have no idea, but it's worth trying." I pressed my fingers on Tavas's neck. He had a faint pulse. "He's still alive, we might as well try."

"We have more of that stuff you used on us after the spider, think we'll need it?" Dima asked.

"Might as well grab it," I said. "Just in case."

"I'll go with you," McKenzie said.

The two of them raced toward our car and Alec slowly walked over to where I was still holding Tavas.

"You sure you want me to try this?" he asked. "We don't know what it will do to a Fae."

Alec's fangs were already showing. The scent of the blood must be too much for him. In the street lamps, Alec looked more pale than usual.

"Are you okay?" I asked.

"I'm fine," he said.

"When was the last time you ate?" I asked. Goosebumps rose on my arms.

"I don't remember," he said. "Before we left."

I took a deep breath and held up my arm, wrist inches from Alec's face, offering my flesh to him. "I need you to heal him. And I need you to be strong enough."

"No." Alec pushed my arm away, then bit down on his own wrist.

Before I could object, he held his wrist over Tavas's mouth and dripped blood over the unconscious man's mouth. Alec lowered his wrist to Tavas's mouth for a moment, then pulled it back. He pressed his palm into his wrist to stop the bleeding.

Without a word, I held up my arm again. "You need to drink."

Alec shook his head. "I told you the day we met that I wouldn't drink from you and I meant it."

"Things are different, this is an emergency," I said.

"We can't have our leader being all woozy from blood loss," he said, pushing my arm away. "I'll be fine."

I was going to object again, but right then, Tavas started coughing. He rolled onto his side and I had to lean over him to keep him from rolling right onto the ground.

My chest was pressed against his torso and I could feel his breath on my cheek as I shifted my position, trying to gently ease him to the ground.

"I didn't realize you cared so much, little dragon," Tavas said.

My cheeks warmed and if I wasn't concerned about hurting him worse than he already was, I would have dropped him. "You know why I'm here."

Finally in a position where I could let go of him, I backed up and looked down at him. His face wasn't as pale as it had been, and his breathing was getting easier.

"I wasn't sure you'd come for me," he said, groaning as he sat up. He looked down at his blood-stained shirt and lifted it up to inspect the wound.

On instinct, I reached out to him, tracing my fingers over the dried blood and his washboard abs. "The cut healed completely."

Tavas looked up at Alec. "I take it this is your doing?"

Alec nodded.

Tavas stretched out a hand. "Thanks, mate."

They shook, Alec looking a bit uncomfortable at the friendly actions of a man that I'd spent the last week hating. Now, he was our only hope for saving our friends.

Dima and McKenzie arrived back at that moment, holding the jar of fennel powder and breathing hard. They must have run all the way back.

"He okay?" Dima asked.

"He's breathing, if that counts," I said.

"He can speak for himself," Tavas said, hoisting himself to

standing. As soon as he set his sight on Dima, he flashed a white-toothed grin. "Why, hello, beautiful."

Dima put her hands on her hips and narrowed her eyes. "Don't even try it. I've heard enough about you."

He shrugged, then turned to me. "So what's the plan, little dragon? I told you that if you saved me, I'd help you."

"James and some other dragon mages were taken," I said.

Tavas lifted an eyebrow. "Other dragon mages? So that's what the whole wild dragon in Realm's Gate thing was all about."

"Seems that way," I said, knowing he was referring to the fact that those with dragon blood didn't get their powers awakened until they were within a short distance of a full grown dragon.

"Whatever we're doing," Alec said, "can we do it away from here? That queen said she'd come check on us and I'd rather get out of here before she returns."

"Smart vamp, this one," Tavas said.

"Yeah, we should go." Without waiting, I started walking toward the car.

My friends and Tavas followed me. I was still torn on having him accompany us. He was untrustworthy, that much was clear. I knew he was capable of using his words to trick anyone he could and I couldn't think of a reason why saving James would benefit him. If I wanted him in my corner, I had to find a way to make him believe that this was good for him.

When we reached our car, I stopped Tavas while the others got inside. He smiled what would have been a charming smile had I not known him.

"Don't give me that look," I said.

"What look? Can't I be grateful that you rescued me?" he asked.

"Grateful?" I scoffed. "You never even said thank you."

"Thank you," he said. "I'm saying it now."

"Right," I said. "Look, I know you don't want to help me. I

know you only agreed so you could help yourself, but I need to hear it from you. I need to know you didn't kill Jimmy. And I need to know that you're not going to turn on me the first chance you get."

"I didn't kill the vamp," he said. "You're going to have to believe me."

"How can I?" I felt anger rising inside me. Chester said it wasn't Tavas, but there was the video showing him and I'd seen him shape-shift before. "It was you on that video, not me. How do you explain that?"

"Ask me how I ended up here tonight, being sentenced to death," he said, all traces of humor gone from his expression.

"Don't change the subject on me, Tavas."

"Ask me," he said. The words came out like a dare, as if he knew I wasn't going to like the answer.

Taking a breath in through my nose, I held back my frustration. "How did you end up here tonight?"

"Because my twin brother got himself mixed up with the Dragon-Bloods, and in Fae law, we're bound to our blood. If a member of our family commits a crime, we're held equally responsible and we all face the same punishment."

"Bullshit." I may have only spent a few hours with Tavas, but I learned my lesson about believing a single word he said.

"It's true," he said. "You know we can't lie. It's a curse."

"You don't have a twin," I said, but doubt was already creeping through me as I watched Tavas's expression.

"We need to go," Alec called from the car. "Whatever is going on here, you figure it out in the car."

"One minute," I said.

"No minutes, now!" Alec pointed.

I turned to look in the direction we'd come from. The dozen Fae guards were headed our way and none of them looked especially happy to see us. Panic shot through me and I pushed Tavas toward the car. "Get in."

Then I ran around to the passenger seat and hopped in. I smacked my hand against the dash to punctuate each word. "Go, go, go."

Alec sped away from the warehouse, twisting and turning down tiny one-way roads lined with run-down buildings and more rusted warehouses. "That didn't look like a friendly visit."

"Something must have changed," I said.

Twisting so I could see the back seat, I locked eyes with Tavas. "This twin thing, you're telling me the truth?"

He nodded, then lifted two fingers in the air. "Scout's honor."

I wrinkled my nose at the human reference. "That doesn't work for you."

He shrugged. "Okay, Fae's honor. Either way, it's true."

"Why were the guards coming after us?" I asked. "Twin trouble?"

"Probably," he said.

"What the hell is going on here?" McKenzie asked. "What is wrong with you people? I was supposed to come along to help you, to protect you, while you rescued some missing mages. I almost died by giant spider, ran from a crazy witch, we just rescued a Fae who was charged with the murder of a vampire crime lord, and now this convict is talking about a twin and he apparently pissed off the Fae guards. And none of it seems to bother any of you?"

I stared at McKenzie, who was wide-eyed and breathing heavy. Part of me wanted to laugh, and part of me wanted to scream back at her. Nobody wanted her here, but she did make a good point. None of this was going as we hoped.

Tavas broke the silence first. By laughing. Alec joined in, then I found myself unable to hold it in anymore and laugher burst from me.

At this point, everyone in the car was laughing, even McKenzie. There wasn't much else we could do. We'd been through hell and hadn't even come close to our objective.

Gasping for air, I finally calmed myself down and wiped off my damp cheeks. "We warned you, McKenzie."

"Right," she said. "Remind me never to go anywhere with you again."

23

"Cheer up, little dragon," Tavas said. "You're about to witness the end of the world."

"What is that supposed to mean?" McKenzie asked.

Moments ago, we'd been laughing, and now it felt like all the joy was sucked out of the air by Tavas's words. He might have a flair for the dramatic, but everything he said had meaning. Those weren't just words to Tavas. If he was saying them, things were far worse than we thought.

"What are you talking about?" I asked. "Does this have something to do with your twin brother?"

"Explain the twin brother thing to me," Alec said.

"I have one, he killed Jimmy," Tavas said, matter-of-factly.

"Right," Alec said. "Of course there's two of you."

"Relax, mate, if it weren't for me, you'd still be in those vampire torture boxes," Tavas said.

"Last I checked, you're not the one who saved him from the box," Dima said.

"Calm down, sweetheart," Tavas said. "We're all on the same team."

"For now," she said.

"Okay, that's enough!" I shouted. "Everyone hates everyone, I get it, but you all have to get over it right now. We have people who are depending on us."

Surprised that I'd said those words, I settled back in my seat. If anyone had a right to be doubtful of Tavas, it was me. But as much as I didn't like it, we were connected in all of this. We had to work together.

I looked at Tavas. "I'm guessing that this is all connected somehow. Your brother, the missing mages, James, the whole end of the world thing, am I right?"

He nodded. "You're bright for a dragon."

Resisting the urge to roll my eyes, I pushed on. "Time to explain. Tell us about the end of the world, and whatever the hell else you know that relates to all of this."

"It's the whole Dragon-Blood ceremony thing," Tavas said as if that explained everything.

"What are you talking about?" I asked.

"Seriously?" He seemed genuinely surprised that his explanation didn't clear everything up. He turned to McKenzie. "Aren't you the head of security for the Mage Order?"

"How do you know that?" she asked.

"You don't think I don't keep tabs on that?" He laughed. "You are terrible at your job, you know that?"

"Hey, there's no reason to be an ass," I said before I realized I was defending McKenzie. Though, between the two of them, I think I preferred McKenzie. She might not like me, but she was honest about that. And she hadn't tried to turn me in to the other side. So far, McKenzie had been almost helpful. Maybe I should lighten up on her.

"Honestly, you mages should know, your order is hiding things from you if they haven't given you this information. I mean, the date has been in the calendar for two hundred years." He shook his head.

Suddenly, the car stopped and I looked out the window to see where we were. Alec stopped at a gas station.

"Why'd you stop?" I asked.

"We're low on gas, and I have to find something to eat," he said.

"Don't look at me," Tavas said from the back seat. "Just because you gave me a donation doesn't mean I'll reciprocate."

"I told you I'd donate," I said.

"No, you can't," Dima said. "You're already weak from teleporting, we can't have you losing blood. I'll do it."

"You sure?" I asked. Giving blood to a vampire was considered an intimate experience. It was something I'd promised myself I'd never do, especially while working for a group of vampires. The last thing I needed was them thinking they could get blood from me any time they wanted. But Alec was my friend and I knew he wouldn't take it the wrong way in our current circumstances.

"Alright, you two lovebirds," Tavas said with a hint of sarcasm. "Why don't we find a place we can lay low for the night and you can do your thing and we can start fresh in the morning."

"We don't have time to stop," I said. "James..."

"James, yes, I get it, love," Tavas said. "But I can't teleport this car back to California. And you are going to get us killed if you attempt to do it twice in one day."

"He's right," McKenzie said.

Tavas smiled at her. "Maybe I was wrong about you."

"Don't even think about it," McKenzie said.

"Fine," I said. "Let's get gas and find the nearest hotel. We'll all rest till first light, then we go save our friends. Right, Tavas?"

"They're not really my friends, but," Tavas began.

"Don't give me that shit," I said. "James is probably the only one who doesn't know how much of a scoundrel you are. If anything, he's the best shot you have at a real friend."

"Oh, little dragon, you forget that we've known each other a long time. James knows exactly what kind of a scoundrel I am."

"Well, I suppose that's why you have to help us, isn't it?" I said.

"Yes, I'll stay. That's what you're getting at, right?" He cocked his head to the side. "You need to get better at asking for what you want."

"Noted," I said as I placed my hand on the door handle. "Tavas, you'll come into the gas station with me in case we have any more trouble."

"I can do it," Alec said.

"No, you stay here and pump gas. The last thing we need is for you to make a snack out of some unsuspecting human." As soon as the words were out, I wished I could take them back. "I'm sorry."

Jaw set, eyes steely, Alec didn't answer. Instead, he stepped out of the car.

"Nice," Tavas said. "Maybe I'll take friendship lessons from you."

"Shut up, Tavas," I said. "Come on."

The two of us walked to the gas station while Alec filled the tank of the car. I let out a long breath as I thought about what I had said to one of the few people in this world I could count on. Alec had been there for me when others failed me. He'd never questioned my innocence when the rest of Realm's Gate was calling me a murderer. And here he was helping me hunt down and rescue a bunch of missing mages and a dragon.

"He'll be fine," Tavas said.

Pausing in front of the glass door to the convenience store, I turned to look at him, brow furrowed in confusion. Was he talking about Alec and the rude comment I'd made or James?

Guilt swirled inside me. I couldn't even feel bad for Alec without my thoughts turning to James. I was a terrible friend.

"Both of them, truth be told," Tavas said.

My blood ran cold. "You're still in my head, aren't you?"

He shrugged. "It's not an easy connection to break."

I whispered a curse under my breath as I pulled open the door to the store.

"It's not so bad," Tavas said. "I mean, I can tell Alec how bad you feel if you want."

I ignored Tavas while I grabbed some bottled water for everyone in the car, then walked up to the counter. "These and gas on pump six."

The plump, older woman behind the counter smiled sweetly as she pulled the bottles closer to her so she could ring them up.

"Why'd you volunteer your blood, anyway? It's not like you have romantic feelings for the guy," Tavas said.

The cashier paused, bottle mid-scan and looked at us like we were crazy people.

"Blood drive," I said.

The excuse helped her relax and she finished scanning the water, stuffing them all into a plastic bag.

I handed her a fifty and waited for my change.

"Anything else I can get for you today?" she asked as she set the bills and coins in my hand.

"Actually, we were wondering if there was a hotel nearby," I said.

"If you make your way through town, you'll find some bed and breakfasts, but I bet they're all full up at this time of night." She looked up and pursed her lips as if thinking hard about this question. "There's something off the freeway, a few miles north. Some chain."

"Thanks," I said, reaching for the bag.

"Have a nice night," the cashier said, pushing our bag of

water closer to us. She still seemed wary of us, but that probably came with the territory of working the night shift at a gas station.

Tavas took the bag from me, then swept his arm out in front of him. "Ladies first."

I glared at him, trying to read into his sudden attempt at being a gentlemen.

"Oh, ease up, Morgan," Tavas said. "I'm just trying to be nice."

His use of my given name startled me, causing me to forget the quip I was going to use on him. Instead, I blinked back in surprise, then turned and walked to the door.

As the door closed behind me, I let out a sigh of relief. No Oracles, no spiders, the gas station hadn't tried to kill us. Maybe there was something to having Tavas tag along that changed the rules.

"How can it not be better with me than without me?" Tavas asked.

I shook my head. "Can we just pretend that you can't read all my thoughts?"

"Sure, love," he said. "But it won't change the fact that I can."

24

We made it to a cheap motel on the side of the freeway. The air was sour, probably a result of whatever they were making in the factory we could see in the distance. I wrinkled my nose, hoping we'd be back to the familiar air of Realm's Gate soon.

As I stood in the parking lot in front of the entrance to our room, I stared at the lights that lit up a factory. There were no sounds or signs of life, just the lights on the tall stacks, illuminating the clouds of smoke rising into the night sky.

It was a vivid reminder that even though it didn't feel possible that I was on the other side of the country, we really were a long way from home.

By the time we got inside the crappy room we'd all share, I was struggling to keep my eyelids open. I didn't like the idea of another detour on this journey, but I knew that magic used your energy. Part of me was surprised I was still standing after everything we'd been through today. I'd always thought of myself as tough, as a survivor, but I'd never been pushed to my limits like this.

The room was minimal, two queen sized beds along a wall, a

chair in the corner, and a small television on a dresser were the only furniture. Every muscle ached and even the brown bedspreads looked inviting.

It was an odd sensation to be walking into a hotel room without a bag. None of us had a change of clothes, or even a toothbrush. Though I think I was tired enough to skip it even if I had brought an overnight bag.

Tavas didn't waste any time stretching out on one of the beds while I stood awkwardly in the center of the room with Dima and Alec.

I heard the deadbolt snap into place behind me and then the sound of the bathroom door closing and knew we'd have a minute or two without McKenzie's interference.

Moving closer to Dima and Alec, I looked at my friends with concern. Alec looked paler than usual, and Dima was still a mess from the spider. "I'm so sorry I dragged you both into this."

"Hey, none of that," Dima said. "We signed up for this."

"No, you didn't," I said. "Not this."

Alec squeezed my upper arm softly. "It's okay. I'm glad I'm here."

I heard the shower start from the bathroom. We had more judgement-free time. "You need to eat."

Dima moved Alec's hand off my arm, then clasped it in hers. "I told you, I'd take care of it."

She walked him over to the chair in the corner, where she sat down. I turned away, not wanting to watch Alec behave like a vampire. The blood drinking thing had always turned my stomach.

"Why don't you sit down." Tavas patted the bed next to him.

I hesitated. Then, Dima let out a moan and I knew Alec was feeding. Wincing, I walked away from my friends over to Tavas and sat down next to him, keeping my back turned away from the vampire's dinner.

"We all have our vices, you know," Tavas said, probably in response to me trying to ignore the discomfort the blood-drinking was causing me.

"Some of us more than others," I said. "You can break this connection, can't you?"

He rested his head on his hands, elbows out. His blonde hair was dirty and streaked with blood but his eyes still sparkled. Despite it all, he hadn't lost that mischievous look in his eye. He stared at me, intensity in his gaze that made me uncomfortable. It was too intimate. Though I supposed there wasn't much he could do that would be more intimate than living inside my head.

"Is that a challenge?" he asked, sitting up so our faces were inches from each other.

I glared at him, heat rising to my face as I felt his warm breath against my skin. "You need to stop this."

"Why?" he asked. "I like being in your head. I can see why James found it so appealing."

Of course he'd know about that, and of course he'd bring it up. "That was different."

"The only difference is that you invited me, he took it." Tavas stretched back down on the bed again as if he couldn't tell that my heart was racing. As if he didn't know that he was getting to me.

I pushed the thoughts away, knowing that nothing inside my head was private. I stood up and stared down at the Fae. "You might have been invited, but I'm asking you to leave, now."

He yawned, covering it lazily. Then, he rolled up to a seated position and shook his head. "I can't."

"Why?" I asked.

"I'm not the one who bound the connection."

"What the hell does that mean?" I asked.

"You know that favor I owed James?" he said with a smile.

"The one you didn't follow through on?" I asked.

He stood, pressing his body against mine. He was trying to make me back down, so I held my ground, unmoving.

Lowering his face so his lips were next to my ear, he whispered, "James connected us while you were in contact with him during that little spell you did. He asked me to keep you safe. If I succeed, I no longer owe him. Of course, if he dies, I no longer owe him."

Before I could react, Tavas slid past me. He went into the bathroom and closed the door behind him. Staring at the closed door, I wondered about this new information. If James was the one who forged this connection, was he the only one who could break it? If something happened to James, if we weren't fast enough to save him, was I going to be stuck with Tavas in my head forever?

Shaking my head, I turned away from the closed bathroom door and the sound of the shower running.

I hadn't even noticed that McKenzie, Dima, and Alec were staring at me in silence. How long were they watching me? Had they been listening to Tavas and me?

Based on the looks on their faces, they'd heard at least part of our conversation. McKenzie's eyebrows were raised in a judging expression. Dima's mouth hung open, and Alec was blinking too much. They were all waiting for me to say something. "I don't want to talk about it."

"So we find out the real reason why we had to rescue this Fae, then?" McKenzie said.

"There is nothing going on between Tavas and me other than an unwanted bond," I said.

"It didn't look so unwanted to me," she said.

"You don't know what you're talking about," Alec said.

Just then, Tavas came out of the bathroom in only a pair of boxers. His long, blonde hair was wet and clean, his skin still damp from the shower. It had been a long time since I'd seen a man in this little clothing and to be honest, he didn't disappoint. He could have passed for a sculpture of a Greek God with his chiseled pectorals and prominent six-pack.

He smiled, the crooked grin of a movie star who knew everyone was checking out his flawless muscles.

Realizing that I was staring, I looked away. "Would you put some clothes on, please?"

"I rinsed them out, they're all wet, besides, I know you don't mind." He walked past me to get to the bed, then pulled the covers down, then sat on the edge of the bed. "Big day tomorrow and I really don't want to die in a bad teleportation spell. Might be time to get some rest."

"Dima, McKenzie, you two can have the other bed. I won't subject either of you to this degenerate," I said.

Tavas settled into the bed, propping his head up on some pillows, still smiling at me.

I stomped over to the tiny closet across from the bathroom and opened it, relieved to find an extra blanket. I tossed it on the bed, then walked to the alarm clock next to the television. It was two in the morning and I could feel the pressure of the time ticking away to get to our friends in time. Knowing I was tired enough to sleep for a solid ten hours, four was going to have to be enough. "Everyone okay with six a.m.?"

A few murmurs of agreement came from behind me as I pushed the buttons on the clock. As tired as I was, it still felt like too much wasted time to stay here and sleep at all. But Tavas's mocking came from a place of truth. I had been successful with the teleportation spell twice now, but history was littered with mages who had hundreds of successful teleportations under their belt and still had the one bad day.

Dima walked by me on her way out of the bathroom. She'd stripped down to a tank top and her underwear and I looked down at my blood and fennel-paste covered clothes. Then, I looked over at my bed-mate for the night. Tavas was unapologetically staring at Dima as she crawled into bed.

Shaking my head, I took my turn in the restroom. I was going to have to live with the dirty clothes for another day.

Clicking off the light, I walked carefully in the dark to the bed where I knew Tavas would be waiting. I really hoped he could handle being a gentleman. Maybe I'd be lucky and he'd be asleep already.

Climbing on top of the covers, I pulled the extra blanket over me and turned so my back was facing the Fae.

"Don't worry, I'll be on my best behavior," Tavas said.

His words came across as sincere. There was none of his mocking tone. I still didn't trust Tavas and I definitely didn't like him, but there was something in the way he spoke those words that made me believe that there might be some good to him somewhere. It was the same feeling I'd had when I let myself trust him in Realm's Gate. James trusted him, so I went along with it. In my naivety, I'd ended up betrayed and nearly captured for a crime I didn't commit.

"Sorry about all that," Tavas said. The words were so quiet, I wondered if I had really heard them.

I knew he could read my thoughts so he knew that even though I was lying there focusing on breathing slowly, I wasn't actually asleep. But I wasn't ready to accept his apology so I said nothing.

The bed rocked and squeaked as Tavas moved around, then all was quiet.

25

*P*anic shot through me as a buzzing sounded from somewhere nearby. It took me a minute to break through the grogginess in the dark to remember that I was in a hotel room and that today was the day. The day we had to save our friends from the Dragon-Bloods and whatever their intentions were.

Someone turned off the buzzing and I turned over in the bed and found myself eye to eye with Tavas.

"Good morning, little dragon," he said. "Sleep well?"

Throwing the blanket off of me, I sat up without responding to him. I felt like I hadn't slept at all. It seemed like only minutes had passed since I turned that alarm clock on.

Alec stood near the television, holding a tray of paper coffee cups. "Good morning."

I smiled at the sight. "You found coffee?"

There were definite perks to keeping a vampire around. He didn't need to sleep so he'd apparently left to find a place where he could get us coffee in time for our early wake up call.

Dima leapt from her bed and grabbed a cup from him, then planted a kiss on his cheek. "You are a saint."

She took a drink. "Not bad."

"How is it, that you of all people, are a morning person?" I knew we had a lot to do but mornings were not my forte.

"Wanna come back to bed?" Tavas asked. "We could cuddle."

"And with that, I'm up," I said, scooting to the end of the bed so I could avoid contact with Tavas.

McKenzie was up now, too. She was moving slower than Dima. "Thanks," she said as she grabbed a cup of coffee from Alec.

Alec set the tray down on the table and pulled one of the cups out, extending it to me.

I took it from him. "You are quickly becoming my favorite vampire."

"I've spent enough time with you now to know how seriously you take coffee. Besides, we need you in top shape today for the teleportation," he said.

My stomach clenched at the words. It wasn't like it was a surprise, that was the plan all along. And it wasn't just the teleportation that was making me nervous, it was the fact that we were going to charge in and try to save our friends from unknown foes today.

"We're going to need a plan," I said, glancing at Tavas.

"Are you asking me for help?" he asked.

I shrugged. "There has to be a reason why you're here, right? I mean, the Oracle said we needed your help and James asked for your help."

"True," he said. "I suppose I should let you all know what you're in for. I mean, it's possible this is the last thing any of us will attempt."

"What is that supposed to mean?" McKenzie said.

"It means that we're going against the Dragon-Bloods on their ritual day, trying to steal one of the two things that were required for their ritual to be successful."

"Explain," I said. "For real this time."

For a moment, Tavas's expression shifted from his usual sardonic smile to a weary frown. Then, he fixed that smile back on his face. "It's the day of the rising. They've been waiting for a long time."

"The rising?" McKenzie asked.

"Right," Tavas said. "I forgot, the Mage Order kept all of this from you. Not a surprise, really."

"Why do you say that?" McKenzie said.

"Stop," I said, holding up my hand to McKenzie. "No side stories this time." I turned to Tavas. "Explain this rising thing. We need to know what we're getting into and how to get our friends out."

"Especially since it seems like they have eyes on us," Dima said.

Tavas lifted an eyebrow. "You think they're tracking you?"

"Possibly," I said. "Keep going."

"I can see why James likes you so much, you're really very alike," Tavas said.

Crossing my arms over my chest, I lifted my eyebrows, silently encouraging Tavas to move on.

"Okay, okay. Give me a second." He stood and walked to the bathroom, coming back out with his pants. He pulled them on, then stood there half-dressed.

I focused on staring at his face, not letting my eyes dip down to his impressive torso.

"The rising is a ritual that can be completed only when the dragon comet is passing by. That's going to happen tonight." He paused, as if waiting for one of us to say something. Nobody spoke.

"They're trying to raise a dragon from the dead," he finished.

"I don't get it," I said. "How do the missing mages and James play into this?"

"Blood sacrifice," Tavas said.

"To raise this dead dragon?" I asked.

"Yes," he said. "You know, to rule the world, conquer everything, that old narrative."

"Seriously?" Dima asked.

Tavas shrugged. "The dragon wars never ended, they've just been biding their time until they could start again."

The hair on my arms stood on end. This was bigger than I feared. This wasn't about people who wanted to play at magic. This was about finishing a war that had started thousands of years ago. Suddenly, all of the fear James had been feeling made sense. If he was part of the key to giving the Dragon-Bloods what they needed to open this conflict back up, his staying hidden was bigger than just wanting to stay out of it.

"Okay, so that's what Chester was talking about," I said, wishing he had been exaggerating. "Now what?"

"We go, we break in, we get them out," Tavas said. "I'm not sure what else you want me to tell you."

"Do you know how many of these Dragon-Bloods we'll find? Or what kind of security they'll have? Or if they have magic or weapons?" McKenzie asked.

"Why would I know that?" he said. "I'm along for the ride as much as the rest of you."

"How are we going to do this?" McKenzie asked.

The alarm buzzed again and I jumped, turning toward it.

"Sorry, had it on sleep instead of off," Alec said, pushing a button on the clock to silence it.

The sound was a reminder. We'd been standing here too long. If we were going to do this, it was now or never. "It doesn't matter. The point is we have to do this."

My friends looked nervous, and I didn't blame them. This is what we had set out to do from the beginning. All the other adventures along the way had been to get us to this point. "It's time."

The tugging sensation from teleporting subsided and I took a deep breath before opening my eyes. Letting out a sigh of relief, I stared out the window at the sight before me. We were in a dirt parking lot surrounded by trees. I hadn't killed us during teleportation.

Leaning back against the seat, I took a moment to calm my nerves. Every time I teleported, it felt more like a gamble. There were only so many times you could get away with doing that before you made a mistake.

If I cast the spell correctly, we were at the Devil's Canyon trailhead in the Angeles National Forest. According to James, there was a mine nearby and we'd find the missing mages there. I hoped he was there, too, though he hadn't told me if he was.

The last thing I wanted to do was crawl into a poorly constructed tunnel left over from the California gold rush, but I didn't come this far to back out now.

"Now what?" Alec asked. He'd sat in the driver seat even though we hadn't started the car.

"We find the mine, I guess," I said.

"Great plan," McKenzie said. "I'm sure that's not going to backfire on us."

"You have a better idea?" I snapped.

"Have you seen the magic Morgan can wield?" Alec said, opening the door. "As long as she's on our side, I'm not worried."

"While I appreciate your confidence in your friend," McKenzie said, "teleporting is hard work. She's probably going to need time to recharge."

Usually, that was the case, but after this round of teleporting,

I didn't feel weakened the way I had in the past. Deciding to test my magic, I whispered a spell and all of the doors to the car flew open.

"Or not," McKenzie said.

"I'm feeling great," I said. "In fact, I haven't felt this energized in a long time."

"Good," Tavas said. "That means we're close."

"How do you know that?" I asked.

"Because when a magic user with dragon blood is around the dragon that awakens them, they get a boost. And it wasn't just James they took. They took my wild dragon, too."

"Wait, these guys are strong enough to capture and hold a wild dragon?" McKenzie asked.

I glanced at the head of security for the Mage Order. Her face was drained of color. She looked afraid.

"You've all heard the stories about the Dragon-Bloods, right?" Tavas said. "Those stories came from somewhere."

"How are we going to do this?" McKenzie asked.

I wasn't sure what prompted me to say it, but the words tumbled out of me, "We split up."

"You can't be serious," Alec said.

I nodded. "I am. We have a better chance if there's two groups of us. That way, if one of us goes down, we have a back up plan."

"But we don't have any plan at all," Dima said.

"That's why it might work," I said. "Remember, they have someone watching us. How can they predict what we're going to do when we don't even know ourselves?"

"I'm not going with him," McKenzie said, staring at Tavas.

Tavas covered his heart with his hand. "Why, head of mage security, are you afraid of me?"

"Stop," I said. "McKenzie, you go with Dima and Alec. Do

whatever it takes to find the missing mages and get them out of here."

"And James?" Dima asked.

"If you find him, get him out, too," I said. "I'll go with Tavas, we'll do the same thing. We don't know where the entrance to the mine is or what security they might have in place."

"If, by some miracle, we succeed, meet back at the car," I said.

"That's great, but how long do we wait and how do we get back if you keep the keys?" McKenzie asked, hands on her hips.

I tossed the keys to McKenzie. "Any mage worth her salt can start a car without the keys. Whoever is here at dusk gets the car. Whoever isn't here is on their own. Got it?"

Silent nods came from my friends. I took a deep breath. "Good luck."

26

"*Y*ou do realize we could have all gone together, don't you?" Tavas asked. "Did you just want some alone time with me?"

"Don't be ridiculous," I said.

"There's something you're not saying," he said.

"I have no idea what you're talking about."

We'd been walking uphill for nearly ten minutes. I stopped and put my hands on my head, taking a moment to catch my breath and look around. All I could see was grass, and stubs, and trees. Nothing that looked like the entrance to a mine. "How are we supposed to find it out here?"

"You know what I'm talking about," Tavas said, ignoring my question. "You split up the group so you could look for James, didn't you?"

"Of course I'm looking for James," I said. "I'm looking for all the missing people."

Tavas shook his head. "Remember, I can read your thoughts. You're hoping they'll do the other job, so you can get your dragon safely."

Guilt twisted my insides. That was exactly what I was

hoping. And in my head, it was a perfectly reasonable idea. Send half the group to rescue the missing mages, and the other half to find the dragon-in-distress. Though I wished Tavas couldn't read my intentions. "Just help me find this mine so we can get this over with before the crazy Dragon-Bloods can perform that stupid ritual."

Tavas shook his head. "You're going about this all wrong, you know that?"

"Your helpfulness never ceases to amaze me," I said.

"Look, you're a mage, right?"

I stared at him, lips pressed together in an annoyed line. Why hadn't I sent Tavas with someone else?

"Why are we looking around here when we both have magic?" he said. "Don't you know any detection spells?"

"None that I can do without knowing more about what I'm looking for," I said. "I'd need a personal item to find someone or some sort of talisman or something I can use to guide me. I can't just make magic happen out of thin air."

"That's true, for mages, but not for dragons. You and James, you think that emotion you feel for him is based on lust alone?" Tavas asked.

Surprisingly, I managed to keep my mind blank in response to Tavas's question. Unfortunately, the flush on my face was giving away my feelings. I crossed my arms over my chest and waited for Tavas to continue.

"You and James spent time together, you're both dragons," Tavas said, as if that cleared everything up.

"And?" I was getting impatient. Was Tavas just trying to distract me? Was he playing me again?

"That means you have a connection that mages don't have, that humans don't have. It's a dragon thing, I'm not sure how it works, but I've been around enough dragons to know that they can find their mate even after years of separation," Tavas said.

"Mate?" My eyes widened. "We just met. There's no mating."

"But you have feelings for him, right?" Tavas insisted. He seemed concerned and frustrated.

"Just tell me what you want me to do, Tavas."

"Find him," he said matter-of-factly.

Eyebrows raised, I blinked at Tavas. "Find him?"

Tavas grabbed my elbow and guided me toward a bench near the trail. "Sit down. Close your eyes."

"You better not be fucking with me, Tavas," I said. "Seriously, there are people's lives on the line here, you know that, right?"

"I know that. And no, I'm not fucking with you. Will you just let me help you? Isn't that why I'm here?"

Relenting, I sat down on the bench and closed my eyes. "Now what?"

"Try a location spell, see if you can find James," he said.

I opened my eyes and looked up at Tavas.

"Just try it, please, what's the harm if I'm wrong?" Tavas asked.

My brow furrowed as I looked up at Tavas's green eyes. He was acting almost like a friend. He wasn't flirting with me or saying anything inappropriate. He wasn't flashing that cheesy smile of his. In fact, his flawless face almost looked worried. Maybe he did care about James. And he was right, there wasn't any harm in trying. Well, aside from him taking off on me while my eyes were closed.

"I'm not going to run off on you," he said. "And believe it or not, I do care about saving James. You were right about one thing, I don't have a lot of friends," Tavas said. "So I need you to just find him, okay?"

"Okay," I said, closing my eyes again. I focused for a moment, recalling all of the variations I knew for detection spells. A seeking spell would be ideal, but the magic needed to find someone over long distances without a talisman or personal item was far too powerful for me to do alone. That was why I'd needed the other mages to help me. But a detection spell might work. It had to.

As soon as I started thinking about the spells, a rush of power surged through me. As if I'd already cast something, without even saying a word. At first, the magic startled me and I almost let it go, then I remembered how I was able to call fire without words. Was this how doing magic would be now that my dragon blood had been awakened?

Instead of focusing on a spell, I held on to the charge of magic inside me and coaxed it along. *James.* Where was he? Would he be able to contact me again? Could I find him the way one would find a missing object? *Where are you?*

Something pulled inside me, causing me to lunge forward on the bench. I opened my eyes and stood, facing the direction of the tugging sensation. Silently, I took a few steps toward it and as I did, it continued, rather than fading like I thought it would.

A smile filled my face and I looked over at Tavas, too happy to care that I didn't like him. "This way."

Jogging, I followed the internal guide as it pulled me off the path, up the mountain, and over a pile of rocks. We crossed a small stream by jumping over it and I was grateful that it wasn't the rainy season right now.

After a few more twists and turns, I lost all sense of where I was or where we had come from. Right now, that didn't matter, what did was finding James and saving him before it was too late.

Suddenly, the feeling vanished. I stopped and looked around, expecting to see some sign that we were in the right place. There was nothing but trees and rocks.

"Everything okay?" Tavas asked.

"It's gone," I said. "What happened? I was being guided and then it stopped."

"We must be in the right place, the entrance has to be around here somewhere," Tavas said.

Behind me, a branch snapped. I turned to look and my mouth dropped open in surprise and I let out a scream. Looking down at me was a ten foot mountain troll.

The creature was the color of gray stones, with mossy green hair. Its skin was rough and had the texture of pebbles. A brown loincloth covered the area between its legs, which made me guess it was a male troll.

Hands the size of trash can lids were pulled into fists and the monster let out a roar that would put a lion to shame.

Terrified, I stood there for a moment, unmoving. What was it that we were supposed to do if we ever saw a troll? A million things raced through my mind at once. They were territorial creatures, usually avoided all contact with the outside world. They liked to be alone and would defend their homes with a vengeance.

Taking a few tentative steps backward, I tried to smile at the creature but I had a feeling it came out as a grimace. "Sorry to bother you, we'll be on our way."

The troll grabbed hold of a nearby tree and pulled it from the ground, roots and all, then held it like a club.

"I don't think he's going to let us go for good behavior," Tavas said.

"You think?" I screamed as I jumped away from the tree that was swung at me. Diving to the ground, I rolled away from a giant foot just as it tried to stomp on me.

"Any bright ideas?" I said.

"One," Tavas said. "Run."

I didn't need to hear it twice and took off through the woods. As soon as I started running, pain exploded through my head and the world began to spin, stopping me in my tracks. A huge gray hand knocked me to the ground and out of the corner of my eye, I saw Tavas fall next to me.

Breathing heavy and dizzy, I fought against the urge to vomit. One gray hand held me to the ground, the other had Tavas pinned. "What now?" I wasn't sure if I actually said the words out loud or if they were only in my head.

The troll squeezed his hand around me, picking me up so I was vertical now, feet hanging in the air. I wanted to say something or do something but my brain was too fuzzy to process a complete thought. The only thing I could think of was that I needed to fight the urge to sleep but my eyes grew heavier with each rocking step the troll took. Then, the world went black.

27

"*M*organ."

From somewhere in the distance, I thought I heard my name, but that wasn't possible. I was alone, in my bed, in my room, wasn't I? But why did everything hurt?

"Morgan."

Head pounding, I opened my eyes slowly as I realized I wasn't at home. The last thing I remembered was being taken down by a troll. This day was not off to a good start.

As my eyes adjusted to the light, the events of the last week came rushing in all at once. The dragon, Jimmy, Tavas, the troll.

Closing my eyes again, I wondered how many times I was going to have to remind myself that this was my life. That this was real.

"Morgan."

For the first time since hearing the sound, I realized who the voice belonged to. My heart raced and I steeled myself against disappointment, not trusting my own ears. "James?" I said his name before I opened my eyes again, afraid that if I opened them, he wouldn't be there.

"I'm here, but I wish you weren't," he said.

At that, my eyes snapped open and I forced my aching body to sit. As my eyes adjusted to the dim light, I realized I was sitting on dirt and the walls around me were made of rock. We were in a cave. "James?"

"I'm here," he said.

Slowly, I turned to look behind me and as soon as I saw him, my chest tightened in a mixture of relief and fear.

James's arms were bound by chains, suspended above his head. His face was bruised and bloody, one eye swollen shut. His dark hair was matted and dirty.

Suddenly, my own pain seemed like nothing. The cave was too low for me to stand, so I crawled over to him, stopping next to him. "What did they do to you?"

He didn't look this bad in the vision when he came to me. Whatever they'd put him through had been recent. The wound on his cheek was fresh, not yet fully closed.

I reached up to touch his face and he turned away from me. "You shouldn't be here. You were supposed to go find the others, not me."

"Did you think I wouldn't come?" I lowered my hand and locked my gaze on his good eye. "You gave up everything to help me. It's my fault you're here in the first place."

He smiled. "That's true, but I still didn't want you to come. I didn't want you to end up in here with me, and look at us now."

"It wasn't just me," I said, brow furrowed. "Tavas was with me. And my friends were looking for the missing mages." I looked behind me, half expecting to see them sitting behind me.

"They didn't bring Tavas or anyone else in here," James said. "But they have no reason to have a Fae. They just want dragon blood."

My stomach twisted. "What does that mean? Do you mean they..." I couldn't finish the sentence. If they were only keeping me because of my ancestry, and they were willing to be this violent with James, someone they needed alive, what chance did Tavas or the others have?

My hands were shaking now. "Did I send all my friends to their death?"

"I don't know," James said.

I knew going in that this was going to be dangerous, but I really thought I could pull it off, though I couldn't explain why I thought it was possible in the first place.

Feeling frustrated, I pressed my fingertips into my temples, trying to ease up some of the throbbing in my head. There had to be a way out of here.

Dropping my hands, I pushed myself up onto my knees and reached up for the chains on James's wrists. The metal was duller and coarser than steel or iron usually was but a simple lock spell should do the trick. "I should be able to get you out of here."

"Don't bother," James said. "It's Fae Iron. Magic won't work on it."

Dropping down, I looked at him. "What is Fae Iron?"

"Just like it sounds, special iron from the Fae Realm. It's toxic to the Fae and can't be broken by magic."

Pursing my lips, I looked back at the chains, then rose back up to my knees. Before James could tell me to stop, I murmured the words for an unlocking spell. It was a simple enough spell that had remained in regular rotation for me when I wanted to investigate things at estate sales. Sometimes, old jewelry boxes or other items were sold while still locked, the keys long gone. It was a spell that worked for me every single time without fail. Until now.

The lock didn't budge. I sat back down, resting my rear on my heels.

"I told you," James said. "I'm stuck here. But you should look around the cave. I've seen a few mice, so there might be a way out somewhere."

I shook my head. "I'm not leaving without you."

"You have to," James said. "You don't know what these people are capable of. There's no way I'm making it out of this alive. The least you can do for me is try to save yourself."

"Did you really think that speech would work?" I asked. "I came here for you."

"Please, Morgan, don't make this harder than it already is," James said. "Go. Maybe you can stop your friends before they end up in the same position."

"I can't," I said, unable to explain why I felt so protective of James. As I'd been telling my friends over and over, we hardly knew each other. But I knew I couldn't leave him here. And as much as I didn't want to admit it to myself, I'd sacrifice all of my friends to get him out of here alive. The thought pained me, and confused me. Why was I so drawn to him?

Before I could stop myself, I straightened up so my face was level with James's, then I pressed my lips against his. He kissed me back with a hunger that went straight to my core, sending heat into every inch of my being. I moved closer to him so our bodies were touching. The tip of his tongue slipped into my mouth and I matched him with mine, licking his lower lip before biting down on it. He pressed back harder, matching my intensity. My whole body felt like it was on fire. Then, he pulled his head away, breaking the kiss, resting his cheek against mine.

Panting, heart racing, I closed my eyes and focused on the moment of intimacy we were sharing by simply being next to one another.

"You shouldn't have come." James sounded just as breathless as me. "But I'm glad you did."

I couldn't help but smile at him, despite the fact that we were both locked in a cave. Carefully, I traced the tip of my finger around his injured eye. "How could someone do this to another person?"

"Don't worry about it," he said.

"But you said they need you alive, why risk hurting you?" I asked.

He leaned his head down so his forehead touched mine. "They caught me talking to you."

"They did this after you came to me?" Once again, James put himself in danger for me. He stared at me and I knew that he felt the connection between us. We needed one another and the Dragon-Bloods were threatening that bond.

I leaned back so I was looking at James. He seemed so fragile right now, chained up like a wild animal, it was something I never thought I'd see. When we first met, he'd had so much strength, so much power.

Anger flashed through me like a wildfire and my jaw tensed. I had to do something. There was no way I was going to sit here and wait until our captors came for us. Both the Oracle and Tavas had mentioned that the ritual would result in the death of the captured. I wasn't going to get this close just to lose everything.

"I know that look," James said. "What are you thinking?"

"I'm thinking that there has to be a way out of here." Crawling on all fours, I explored the dim cave. Behind us, the cave narrowed until it reached a natural wall that closed us off.

I turned around and crawled the opposite direction, expecting to find an entrance guarded by Dragon-Bloods or sealed off with a door or bars. Instead, I found more walls. My throat tightened as I realized we were surrounded by stone. There was no way out. Had they sealed it with magic? If so, there had to be a spell I could do to get it to open.

"How the hell did we get in here?" I asked.

James lifted his chin and I followed his gaze. Above us, there was a narrow oculus in the ceiling that I hadn't noticed before.

I crawled to the space right below the opening and peered upward. There was a column of darkness that extended above us. It was the only place in the entire room that was high enough for me to straighten to my full height. But the opening was narrow, too small for me to fit more than my head inside, let alone James.

"How? What spell did they use?" I said the words more for myself than anyone else. Growing up around magic, there was little that I deemed impossible. But I didn't know any spell that could make stone shrink or grow or move without serious consequences. If you altered the structure of a place like this and didn't do it correctly, it was possible the whole thing could cave in.

Ducking down, I walked back over to James. "That's it, we're teleporting out of here."

I wasn't sure why I hadn't thought of it before. I should be able to focus the spell so that I teleport him out without the chains. It should work and it was worth the risk if the alternative was death.

James shook his head. "It won't work for me, Fae Iron." A sad smile tugged at his lips. "But you should go. You can get free of this place, go home, have a life."

"You know I won't do that," I said. "Besides, Tavas made it sound like there won't be much of a life to live if these Dragon-Bloods get what they want." I settled on the ground, cross-legged, next to him.

"That's true," he said.

"Is this why you were hiding?" I asked.

"They needed the blood of an elite for their ritual," he said. "I'm one of the few that remain. And one of the few who oppose their cause, so I'm an ideal sacrifice."

"What's going to happen? They won't kill you in here, right?" Prickles of fear traveled down my spine as I resigned myself to the possibility that I wasn't going to survive this. The only chance we might have was if they removed us from this cave for whatever was needed for the ritual.

"They won't kill me in here. They'll come for me." He lowered his voice. "Probably for you, too."

"Then what?" I had to hope there was something. A step in the process we could exploit.

"They'll take us to the burial site."

I didn't like the sound of that. "What burial site?"

"Where the Dragon Queen was buried. They have to perform the ritual there."

"Is it nearby?" I asked, hoping for a long transport where we could buy ourselves some time.

"Right on top of this mountain," James said.

"What happens if they wake up this queen?" I asked.

"The dragons will return to this realm," James took a breath, "and they'll kill anyone and everything that stands in their way."

28

"We can't let this happen." I put my hands on James's thigh and leaned in to him. "We have to get away from them before they can complete the ritual. Stop it somehow."

"I don't think that's going to happen," a new voice said from behind me.

How had someone managed to get in here? I turned with a start and then my shoulders relaxed in relief. "You're okay."

I was surprised how happy I was to see the troublesome Fae. "How did you get in here? Did you find the way out?"

"I think you must be mistaking me for someone else," he said. "You see, that happens sometimes, though I think I'm much better looking than that brother of mine."

My breath caught in my chest as the realization sunk in. "You're not Tavas."

"Jaret, let her go. Haven't you used her enough already?" James said.

"Under normal circumstances, I might be inclined to approve the last request of a condemned man. However, one of our dragon mages was killed trying to escape and we are short one for the ritual. So, now your girlfriend gets to join in the fun. It's rather romantic, really. The two of you sacrificing yourselves for the rise of the dragons."

James pulled at the chains, trying to break free of the wall. "Jaret, you son of a bitch, you let her go."

"What are you going to do about it?" Jaret said with a sneer.

Not only was the man responsible for taking James and the others, he was the one who killed Jimmy. He was responsible for the destruction of Realm's Gate by dragon. If anyone deserved to die, it was him.

James might be trapped in here, but I wasn't. Moving as fast as I could while doubled over in the low cave, I charged at the newcomer.

Just as I was about to crash into him, an invisible force hit me, knocking me backward. I landed next to James, feeling disorientated, but determined to get back up. Moving slower than I wanted to, I fought to right myself, eyes narrowed at Jimmy's murderer.

Nostrils flaring, I opened my palms, fingers wide, and thought of fire. If I couldn't fight him, I'd burn him to death.

Flames roared to life in my hands, spreading up my wrists. Lifting my hands, I aimed at Jaret.

Then, from out of nowhere, the flames died. I tried to lift my hands so I could see them, but they were paralyzed in front of me. I tried to move my head so I could look down, but my body wouldn't respond to me. I was stuck. "What did you do?"

"You should know better than that," Jaret said. "No mage is a match for a Fae. Not even one with dragon blood."

"You're a murderer," I said, fighting the tears that stung the back of my eyes. Here I was, face to face with Jimmy's killer and I was useless to defend myself, let alone avenge his death.

Jaret rolled his eyes. "So attached to others, so emotional. Just like that no good brother of mine."

With a lazy wave of his hand, Jaret sent my sliding across the ground, until I slammed into James. My head throbbed harder than it had before and I reached up to rub my forehead. This time, my body responded. I could move again, but I knew I was going to have to be smarter about attacking Jaret. I wasn't strong enough to do it on my own.

"You're going to regret this, Jaret," James said.

"Oh?" Jaret stood under the oculus, a smile on his face. "I don't think I will."

"You think the dragon queen is going to keep you on as her second? Her mate? You're nothing to her. She'll probably eat you," James said.

"It's possible," Jaret said. "But you and I know what it's like to live longer than we need. The world won't mourn either of us. It's just a shame your young protege won't get to enjoy the benefits of old age."

"I hope that dragon eats you slowly," I spat.

"I'm sure you do," he said.

A moment later, he rose into the air and vanished into the opening on the ceiling.

I raced over to it, hoping it was still wide enough for me to climb through, but it wasn't any larger than it had been before he arrived.

Angry and confused, I lost the battle to keep the tears hidden and they streaked down my cheeks. I turned to James. "We have to stop them."

He was silent for a moment but looked like he was thinking of how to respond to me so I didn't press him.

After a moment, James took a deep breath, then let it out slowly. "When they come for us, they're going to ask you to drink something. I'm going to need you to take it from them. Don't fight it."

I turned away from him, not believing my ears as more tears

welled up in my eyes. Was he asking me to give up? This was it, then. No fighting back, no way to defend ourselves. Just give in. "How could you say that. There has to be something we can do."

"Look at me, Morgan."

Hesitantly, I turned to face him, not hiding the disappointment on my face.

"They won't kill you at the beginning of the ritual, they'll keep as many of you alive as possible to offer as sacrifices to the queen when she rises. They just need your blood. But if you resist, they'll kill you for sure. If you play along, you can run once the ritual starts." He didn't look as confident as I would have liked, but his words sounded sincere.

"What does the drink do?" I asked.

He looked away and a flush of embarrassment filled his face. "It's the same thing I gave you at my house."

"But I don't even remember that, how can I escape if I'm under the control of that drink? And how does that help you, or the others? I can't take it."

"You won't have a choice. If you don't take it, they'll kill you. And if you don't escape, you'll die," he said.

"That's my only hope? That they don't kill me too quickly? And then I'm supposed to leave you and everyone else behind?" After everything, that was it. Give up and let someone else save me? "I can't."

"You can. You're strong enough to fight it. You have to fight it."

I shook my head and walked back over to him, sitting down next to him. I reached a hand out to stroke his cheek with my fingers. "I'm not leaving you behind. When they come to get us, they'll have to remove your chains. We can fight them together."

He leaned his cheek against my hand. "No, we can't. They have a weapon that I can't fight."

"What kind of weapon?" I asked.

"They can force me to shift and in my dragon form, I'm not me. I don't think like me. I don't have control," he said.

"We have to try," I said.

"Forgive me," James said.

I pulled my hand away, brow furrowed. "For what?"

"I'm cashing in my favor," James said.

Panic welled up inside me. "No, don't do this."

"Morgan, I have a favor to ask you," he said the words over my protests. "When the Dragon-Bloods come for us, I need you to take the drink, but resist the herbs. I need you to not let them get to you."

An icy chill fell over me and my lower lip trembled. This had to be the feeling of a bargain being set in place. When they came, I'd have no choice. I'd have to take the drink, and I had to hope that his words were enough for me to resist the effects of the herbs. "Why?"

James opened his mouth to speak, then closed it, his gaze leaving mine to something beyond me.

Turning around, I saw what caused him to lose focus. We were no longer alone in the cave. Jaret was back, and this time, he had company. Six hooded figures stood behind him, their cloaks covering their eyes so I couldn't make out the features of their faces.

"It's time," Jaret said.

One of the figures took a step forward, and dropped the hood. My mouth dropped open in shock as I stared at Jasmine, the head of the Mage Order. Chester was right. I knew at least one person in the Dragon-Bloods.

Closing my mouth, I scowled at her. "I should have known you'd have something to do with this."

"I'm sorry you have to get involved like this," she said. "McKenzie was supposed to lead you off track, keep you away from here. I thought I'd made that clear to her. But her sense of nobility kicked in, I suppose."

"I don't get it," I said. "If you wanted me dead, why not just kill me before?"

"Don't you get it?" she asked. "I really didn't want you dead. I'd never have given you that journal from your mother if I did."

In the chaos of the last few days, I'd forgotten about the journal. It was tucked somewhere in Dima's car. I hoped my friends had failed to find anything and were on their way back to that car right now. Maybe Dima or Alec would have the good sense to hide the journal for me.

"I wanted your help with all of this, but I knew I'd have to win your trust slowly. So I let you go on your quest, figuring we could keep you away long enough. But you bested our seer," Jasmine said.

Another figure stepped forward. "I never thought you'd go to the Oracle, let alone agree to work with Tavas."

I knew that voice and without realizing what I was doing, I scrambled back, trying to distance myself from the group. I was an adult now, I was no longer a child, but the voice of my past tormentor brought me right back to that place of fear.

"Morgan," James spoke behind me, but his voice sounded far away.

My hands trembled as I watched the man drop his hood, but I already knew what I would see.

"It's nice to see you, again, Ladybug." Dr. Byers's dark eyes stared back at me. He smiled, as if he didn't care that he'd broken my trust for anyone with telepathic powers. As if he didn't care that I'd spent years fearing that he'd return and continue his unethical studies on me and the other mage children he managed to rope into his courses.

Imagine spending two hours every week with someone inside your head. Controlling all of your actions. Imagine walking around town aware of everything but unable to respond in the way you wanted to. For two years, I was his puppet and there was nobody else in this world I hated more than him. "Don't call me that, you sadistic fuck."

Dr. Byers smiled. "It wasn't all bad, was it?"

"Fuck you," I said.

Someone handed him a vial of liquid and he passed it off to Jasmine. "You better give it to her. She might bite off my hand it I get too close."

Jasmine took the liquid without a word and walked over to me. "Don't worry, dear. It'll be over soon. And you won't remember a thing."

I wanted to fight it. I didn't want to take the drink. Tears of frustration prickled at the back of my eyes.

Jasmine reached her hand out, the vial of liquid in her hand. "Go on, take it. Don't make me hurt you."

Every muscle was on fire as I resisted taking the drink. I knew the longer I waited to fulfill the favor, the worse it would get.

"Go ahead," James said, his words gentle.

Closing my eyes, I gave in, and reached my hand out. The vial was placed against my palm and I closed my fingers around it.

Without opening my eyes, I lifted it to my lips, then threw my head back as I tipped in the contents.

29

_T_he liquid tasted sweet on my tongue, different than it had in the tea James gave me when we first met. My instincts told me to spit it in Jasmine's face, but the thought was fleeting, and I swallowed it.

"See, that wasn't so bad," Jasmine said.

I glanced back at James, letting him know with my expression that I wasn't pleased with what he'd made me do.

"Don't worry about him," Jasmine said. "We've got big plans for both of you. But right now, it's your turn. Follow me."

It took me a moment to realize that I was following Jasmine without considering my actions. The drink was already kicking in, making me do things I didn't want to do. Somehow, the oculus above us expanded and I was pulled upward, landing inside another, wider cave. Jasmine continued walking, the other Dragon-Bloods behind me, and I continued to follow without question.

James's attempt at helping me resist didn't seem to work. Anxiety fluttered in the pit of my stomach and I wondered if I was going to willingly follow Jasmine and the others to my death.

Then, while still following Jasmine as she lead us down a stone corridor lined with torches, I realized that I was aware of what was going on. This didn't feel like the herbs James gave me in the tea. When I took that, I lost all awareness. This was more like what happened when Dr. Byers had pulled on the strings of my mind, making me do things without my consent. What did that mean? Was there a way to break through? As a child, I wasn't able to reclaim control. It took me running from sessions for weeks before my mom stopped making me go.

Was there a way I could do it now? I wondered if there was anything in the book my mom left behind. Was there anything I could have learned from that before I charged in to this?

Ahead, I saw a column of sunlight pouring into the cave from above. As I neared the opening, it expanded, growing wide enough for five people to rise through at once. On the edges of the opening, I noticed the loose boards and rotting structure. We were at the old entrance to the mine. So the room I'd been in with James must have been an old mining tunnel. Somehow, they were using magic to control the openings to the tunnels.

"Out here," Jasmine's voice carried in from the other side of the cave. I'd slowed down, taken my time. Did that mean I could resist her orders? Wanting to see if it was possible, I willed myself to stop walking. My legs continued to move, despite my mind screaming for them to cease.

For a moment, I wondered if it mattered. If I couldn't save my friends, if the world was about to end in dragon fire, anyway, did it matter if I escaped? What kind of escape would that be? Get away just long enough to watch the world burn, alone and full of regret?

Jasmine stopped in front of a circular hole in the mountainside. She pointed to the spot next to her. "Stand right here."

I took the position she indicated and stopped moving. Glancing down, I looked at the hole. It looked like it went straight through the mountain, dark and forbidding, I couldn't see the end. It reminded me of the hole I'd jumped into with James that took us to his secret garage, but I had a feeling I wouldn't like where this hole ended.

"Let me go, you brute."

I turned at the sound of a familiar voice and saw Dima being led in with McKenzie and Tavas. Each of them was held by two guards. "Where's Alec?"

Dima shook her head. "I don't know. We got separated."

"What did you say?" Jasmine asked. "You shouldn't be asking questions."

I pressed my lips together. Had I just given away my advantage?

Jasmine looked at me, eyes narrowed. "I suppose it doesn't matter if you're aware. It'll just hurt more when I slice your throat."

"You crazy bitch," McKenzie said. "How could you do this to us? To the Order? I trusted you. I followed you."

"Why do you think I gave you the security position?" Jasmine said to her former employee. "You wanted to belong so bad, you missed all the details. Think of all those nights I asked you to reset the cameras or clear the old data."

McKenzie looked away from Jasmine and my heart ached for her. She'd been played in all this just as much as I had.

Looking away from McKenzie, my eyes settled on Tavas. He had caused me pain in the past, but now I had a feeling that I didn't know the whole story. While I still didn't trust the Fae, he probably wasn't as bad as I thought he was.

Suddenly, I felt a searing pain slice through my arm and I turned away from my friends as I cried out. Jasmine was backing away from me, a knife stained with blood in her hand.

Breathless, I looked down to see the cut on my forearm. Blood rolled down my arm and onto the ground below.

"Stop it!" someone screamed from behind me. "Let her go!"

Jasmine grabbed me by my wrist and pulled my arm over the hole in the ground. With a ruthless squeeze, she wrapped her fingers around my arm and caused the bleeding to increase so my blood fell into the hole.

I wanted to pull away, to resist, but I was frozen there. Forced to endure everything she was doing to me. My arm throbbed from where her fingers had pressed into my flesh and the slice across my skin stung.

Apparently finished with me, she dropped my arm and took a step back. From somewhere behind me, a hooded figure emerged, leading a group of three bound young women with blank eyes. They paraded by us, one at a time and I watched, helpless as all three women I didn't know were cut open by Jasmine, and had their blood squeezed into the chasm below.

After they were finished, their captor dragged them away, where they stood in silence, watching and waiting for whatever was going to happen next. None of them seemed aware of their surroundings. Each woman stood motionless, their arms at their side, blood dripping to the ground from a wound they didn't seem to feel.

Then, another hooded figure guided three more mindless women to the tunnel. My heart raced as I recognized the beautiful red-head at the back of the group. "Lyla!"

Jasmine looked up from the first of her new round of victims, knife in mid-slice and glared at me. Then, she smiled, and went back to adding more blood to the hole.

It was a horrible sight, and with each new wound, bile rose in my throat. How could someone be so terrible? "You know this isn't going to be good for you in the end, right?"

Jasmine cut open Lyla's arm and dragged my unaware friend for her blood donation in the twisted ritual we'd all become a part of.

"There will be rewards for those of us who help the dragon queen rise," Jasmine said. "Don't worry, we'll let you live long enough to see her rebirth. Then, she can eat all you lovely maidens as tribute to her greatness."

"That's the plan?" I said. "You're going to feed us to a dragon?"

Dying as dragon food sounded like a terrible way to go.

Desperate to figure out a way out of this, I looked around again. Dima, Tavas, and McKenzie stood by watching all of this happen. I wondered if they'd been drugged too. Part of me wanted to point out that they shouldn't be there. That they might anger the dragon queen if she was looking for those with dragon blood as her tributes, but I had enough sense to realize that that could lead to their immediate execution.

"Please, you got your blood. Just let us go." It was worth a try. I might not have the ability to walk away, but I could argue.

Jasmine lifted her chin toward me and before I could process why, a pair of hands pressed against each of my arms. Looking behind me, I realized I was now being held by Jaret.

"Why are you even here?" I asked Tavas's evil twin. "What's the point of you in all of this? You're not even a dragon blood."

He smiled. "We do crazy things for those we love, don't we?" He was staring at Jasmine.

"Seriously? Her?" The words were out of my mouth before I thought them through.

"I'm going to pretend you didn't just insult the love of my life," he said, squeezing my arms tighter.

Jasmine lifted her hands into the air, not letting my words break her focus. I had to give it to her, she was good at ignoring me.

"Goddess, mother, father, moon," Jasmine began an incantation. "Today we seek the return of your child, wrongfully imprisoned by the weak minded. The mother to us all, the mother of greatest creature the goddess created. The mother of all the dragons."

My mind was racing as I tried to think of what I could say or do to stop this. What spell did I know that could block someone else's magic? I tried to think of what I had learned but no magic came to me. It was like I was hitting an invisible wall in my own mind, preventing me from accessing the part of me that kept magic. My chest tightened in frustration. How was I supposed to stop this? If the dragon was raised, we were all dead.

"Mother, please accept our sacrifice to you," Jasmine said, holding up the knife.

A roar vibrated under me, shaking the mountain we stood on. Then, from the black pit of the hole, the place where my blood and the blood of the other six women had been spilled, fire came rushing out.

I stiffened and my eyes widened. This was the end. It was too late. I was about to be dragon food.

A rush of wind whipped my hair around my face as something emerged from the hole. Somehow, through that small opening, a full grown dragon rose, wings spread. It opened its mouth to let out another roar and released fire on Jasmine.

Her clothes caught in flames and she patted them down, without flinching. Like me, Jasmine seemed immune to dragon fire.

My heart thundered in my ears and fear crawled across my skin as I stared at the beast. It turned to look at me, amber eyes locked on mine. "James?"

Nobody could hear me over the thrashing and noise that James was making in his dragon from. He was suspended above the opening, an unwilling participant in all of this, just like me.

Jasmine walked over to him, her knife raised. "And with this last sacrifice, mother, we call you forward."

"No!" I screamed just as Jasmine jammed the blade into the

side of the dragon. The beast let out a roar of protest and I tried to run to James. The edges of my vision blurred as hatred pulsed in my temples. I wanted to get that knife and shove it in Jasmine's heart. I wanted to watch her let out her last breath.

Instead, I cried out again as shooting pain in my ears spread to my forehead and behind my eyes.

*S*queezing my eyes shut, I fought the pain. It was as if something was digging through my head and moving around in there.

Stop fighting me. The words seemed far away and I couldn't tell if they were inside my head or if they were being spoken by someone standing around the tunnel.

Damnit, little dragon. Let me in.

My breath caught. I knew that voice and I'd been fighting to get him out of my head. Now, Tavas was speaking to me through the connection we'd forged.

Head throbbing, I focused on relaxing as much as I could. Maybe Tavas had a way to stop this. Something he could do to help us or save James.

I'm trying to break down the hold the herb has. Then you can save me.

I frowned. Of course he'd want me to save him. Wait, why was an all-powerful Fae standing there captured in the first place? And where was Alec? And what the hell was going on here? The more I wondered about the situation, the less I focused on what was happening from Tavas inside my head. I almost forgot he was there and the pain was easing.

Try to move.

Taking a deep breath, I opened my eyes. My head wasn't hurting anymore. Did that mean Tavas had broken through? Starting with my foot, I edged my toe forward, just to see if it responded.

My foot slid forward, the way it should, without any effort. My breathing picked up and my heart pounded. This was it, I was free. Knowing that I'd likely be stopped by Jasmine or the other Dragon-Bloods, I knew I'd only have one shot. I could try to break McKenzie, Dima, or Tavas free. Or I could go for James.

Like I have to even ask what you're going to do.

Tavas was right, my first instinct was to go to the wounded dragon flapping his wings and howling in front of me, but what would I be able to accomplish by that? I might be able to save him, but it was more likely a last ditch heroic act that would end up costing both of us.

I knew what I needed to do. Chester had sent me after Tavas for a reason. Probably because he could break the control of the herbs on my willpower, but it had to be bigger than that.

If Tavas had any good in him, this was his chance to prove it.

Hoping I'd made the right decision, I twisted away from Jaret, who was so focused on the scene ahead of him, he hadn't noticed the changes in my behavior.

Breaking away at a sprint, I ran toward Jaret's mirror image while he lunged after me. In a rush, I whispered the words to the binding spell, aiming the bright green strands of magic at the feet of the hooded Dragon-Blood I was charging.

I rushed the Dragon-Blood holding Tavas and as the startled man let go of Tavas to defend himself against me, he tripped on the bindings around his feet and landed on the ground.

"Help me," I called to Tavas as I used the same binding spell on the Dragon-Blood holding McKenzie. He went down surprisingly quickly and both of the incapacitated Dragon-Bloods rolled around on the ground, but didn't attack me with magic. I wondered if they could.

"McKenzie, take out the Dragon-Bloods," I shouted.

The freed mage didn't waste any time and joined me in creating destruction as best we could to incapacitate the other Dragon-Bloods.

"Stop them!" Jasmine cried. "Don't let the ritual break."

Shoving over a bound guard, I looked over at Jasmine. There was a purple light extending from her that surrounded James. Had that been there the whole time or was it something new?

I stared at the glowing light. "What the - ugh." A hooded Dragon-Blood knocked me to the ground and I landed with a thud.

Angry at being thrown down, heat twisted through me, simmering somewhere deep within. This time, I didn't stop it. A rush of fire came flooding from my hands, engulfing the Dragon-Blood in flames.

I heard him screaming as I rolled away from him, then the screaming stopped. A burning pile of robes and the smell of singed hair filled the air. The Dragon-Blood wasn't resistant to fire and like the others, he hadn't used magic to fight me. He wasn't part dragon. And he wasn't a mage. Had Jasmine convinced a bunch of humans to help her?

Scrambling to my feet, I found Tavas, who was guiding a few of the kidnapped girls away from the fight. For a moment, I let myself smile. He was helping us. Then, I looked around for McKenzie and Dima.

Dima was standing at the distance, hands out in front of her like claws in a defensive position, daring someone to come after her. McKenzie was nearby, engaging in hand to hand combat with another Dragon-Blood who had thrown the cloak to the ground.

The fighter was a young woman who seemed well trained in combat, but wasn't using any magic to retaliate. After a quick glance to make sure I wasn't going to get jumped again, I searched for magical signatures. The whole mountain top was vibrating with magic, but none came from the woman McKenzie was fighting.

Quickly, I called out another binding spell and sent the magical tendrils to capture McKenzie's opponent.

The woman fell to the ground, struggling against her invisible bonds.

McKenzie looked up at me. "I had that." Her face was flushed and she was breathing heavy.

"You did, but you're not using your magic, you're wasting time. They're humans. They don't have any magic," I shouted.

"Jaret, do something," Jasmine called.

Expecting to see the Fae man charging at me, I squeezed my hands into fists instinctively. Instead, I noticed a flicker out of the corner of my eye as Jaret ran past me from wherever he had been waiting.

The Fae raced by McKenzie, past Dima, and finally slowed to a stop in front of Tavas.

"Get these girls out of here," Tavas said. "I'll take care of my brother."

"Dima," I shouted, happy to see she'd already headed in that direction before I called to her.

"McKenzie, help get them out," I said.

"What about you?" she asked.

"I've got to try to stop this thing." We'd managed to disable the Dragon-Bloods, who aside from Jasmine and the missing Dr. Byers, were nothing but humans she must have convinced to join her.

"Good luck," McKenzie called out as she took off.

Now it was my turn. Jaw tense, I started toward Jasmine.

"It's too late," the crazed mage called out to me. Her hair whipped around her face as the power from the ritual seemed to charge through her. It was as if Jasmine was the conduit for the whole thing and a glowing light connected her to the distraught dragon still hovering above the hole.

How was it that he hadn't flown away yet? What had she done to him? When I pulled that knife from him, would it end this whole thing?

I didn't know what I was supposed to do, but I knew I didn't want her to win and I didn't want James to die.

The ground under me shook, forcing me to halt my progress toward the crazy mage. A crack shot through the mountaintop, sending a split in the surface from the hole, past Jasmine and into the distance.

Jasmine cackled, raising her hands into the air. She looked like a cartoon mad scientist. A blinding light radiated from her and I had to turn away to shield my eyes.

When I looked back, the dragon was gone and Jasmine was lying flat on the ground, unmoving.

A few feet away from where Jasmine lay, I saw a second figure. My heart pounded against my ribs. "James!"

I could still see the knife in his side, but just like Jasmine, he was on the ground, in human form, not moving.

The ground continued to shake and I stretched my arms out for balance, running forward. Leaping over the prone form of Jasmine, I dropped to my knees at James's side. I pressed my fingers to his neck feeling for a pulse. His heartbeat throbbed against my fingers and I blew out a breath of relief.

The ground rumbled harder and more cracks expanded outward like ripples from the hole. I grabbed James under his arms and dragged him away, worried that the ground was going to give way. Just as we reached a patch of large shrubs, an explosion of rock and dust shot forth from the center of the mountain.

Through the cloud of debris, I saw Jasmine's body slide into the gaping hole just as a massive black dragon shot into the sky.

The beast flapped iridescent wings that sparkled like stardust as it opened its mouth to let out a deafening roar.

For a moment, the creature hovered in the air above the mountain, beating its massive wings to stay afloat. It looked at me, and it felt like a dart of ice went right through my heart. I gasped, unable to take my eyes of the dragon queen. Intense pain radiated from my chest, into my neck and arms, all the way to my fingertips. Then, it stopped. My breathing returned to normal and I continued to stare into the brilliant blue eyes of the graceful winged beast in front of me.

She regarded me with a calmness I hadn't expected. Wasn't she supposed to eat me? I wanted to shrink away from her, run, or hide, but I couldn't make myself act on those instincts. It was as if something internal was overriding my sense of fight or flight and I just waited, staring at her in all her beauty.

A grunting sound broke the silence that had settled between the two of us and we both turned toward the noise. Tavas and his brother, Jaret were still engaged in combat. The two of them throwing punches and dodging blows. I had a feeling that they could be using magic to fight, but there was something primal and personal about the combat between the two Fae.

If not for the clothing Tavas had on, I wouldn't have known which man was which. Their faces were identical, save for the streaks of blood and bruises taking up different positions on each of the brothers.

The Dragon Queen let out a screech that stilled the men. They stopped fighting and Tavas dropped his guard, staring up at the dragon in awe. He dropped to his knees, as if it prayer.

Jaret let out what was probably supposed to be a celebratory cry.

In a flash of midnight wings, the Dragon Queen descended on the two Fae.

Jaret's cries of joy turned to a choked yelp of fear while Tavas remained in place, head lowered in submission.

I should have felt fear as the dragon swooped in on Tavas, or some twisted sense of satisfaction at him getting payback. But I found myself devoid of emotion, no fear, no joy, nothing. Just a blank slate studying the way her muscles moved, the way she flapped the giant wings, the way she gracefully threw back her head to call out a warning before she clamped down on Jaret with her massive jaws.

The man's cries were instantly cut short as the Dragon Queen carried her meal away and I watched, feeling a sense of peace wash over me as she did. Unmoving, I continued to stare into the sky until the wings were small black specks flying through the air.

Gone from view, sadness overtook me and I wondered when I would be able to see the magnificent creature again.

31

"*M*organ," Tavas called to me, breaking my trance.

I looked down from the sky over at the bloody and bruised fae.

"We gotta go," Tavas said. "Come on, before she comes back for dessert."

Nodding, I leaned down to where James still lay unconscious. The knife embedded in his side. I might not be a healer, but I knew enough about first aid to know that you don't pull something out of someone until you're in a position to stop the blood flow that will pour from a wound like that.

A grunting noise drew my attention away from James for a moment, and I looked over at one of the bound Dragon-Bloods. My nose scrunched up in disgust. They weren't even mages. They probably didn't even have dragon blood. How had Jasmine gotten them all involved?

Tavas was standing next to me now, and he knelt down to check on James. "He's hurt badly, but if we can get him to a healer, I think we can save him."

Gently, Tavas hoisted James over his shoulders, somehow balancing the six-foot man over his own tall frame. "Come on."

I took a few steps, then stopped, looking back one more time at the two remaining humans who hadn't burned to death and avoided falling into the gaping chasm that remained at the top of the mountain after the rising of the dragon queen. "What about them?"

Tavas glanced over his shoulder as best he could with James on top of him. "The humans? What about them?"

"Do we just leave them here to starve and die?" I asked, a surprising twinge of guilt flashing through me.

"What do you want us to do? Let them go so they can run to the dragon queen?" Tavas asked.

Quickly, I whispered the unbinding spell on the person nearest me.

With a gasp, the freed Dragon-Blood, or whatever he was, rubbed his mouth in relief. "Thank you."

"Why did you help Jasmine?" I asked.

"Now's not really the time," Tavas said, a touch of strain in his voice.

I ignored him, silently giving the person in front of me twenty seconds to give a good enough excuse before I released my fire.

"She said she'd help us gain powers," the human said. With the hood lowered and the fanfare of the ritual gone, he looked broken and pathetic.

"You don't deserve powers," I said. "You know that, right?"

He lowered his head, unable to make eye contact with me.

"If I ever see you again, I will kill you," I said.

"She won't have a chance to kill you because I'll get to you first if you set one toe out of line," Tavas said.

Surprised that he joined the conversation, I almost smiled, but managed to keep a stern look on my face.

As I turned away from the defeated man, I released the other person from their binding. "Take care of your friend, and pass our message along."

"I will, thank you for your mercy."

Tavas and I walked down the mountain in silence. I knew fae were strong, but he'd been through a lot, and his breathing was uneven as he carried James down.

"Can I do anything to help?" I asked, knowing I couldn't carry James but not wanting to feel so useless.

"Not right now," Tavas said.

"Thank you, by the way," I said.

He smirked. "You're welcome."

It was strange how comfortable the silence between us felt as we continued our careful descent. It was as if most of my hatred toward Tavas had been removed, possibly even replaced by mild affection. How had that happened?

"Thanks," Tavas said. "Right back at ya, little dragon."

Instead of feeling annoyed that he was still in my head, I chuckled. "I might not hate you anymore, but I have to say that I'm looking forward to getting you out of my head."

"As soon as we have this guy fixed up, I'm sure he'll break the bond. There's no way he'll want me in your head for a reunion between the two of you."

Heat rushed to my neck and cheeks as I recalled the kiss James and I shared in the cave. There was no way I could deny my feelings for James, no matter how quickly they'd grown. Getting to spend time with him alone, while safe was worth fighting for. The comfortable image of the two of us shattered before it was even fully formed in my mind.

Even if we got James to safety, even if he recovered, there was still a giant dragon on the loose that was supposedly set on bringing destruction to the rest of the world. "What happens now?"

Tavas didn't need more details. Considering he could probably hear all the fear swirling in my mind as images of the massive beast swallowing his brother whole flashed through my head.

"We can't think about that right now. Jasmine is gone, so is Jaret." He said the words without even the slightest sense of sorrow.

I didn't have any siblings, but I wondered how terrible it had to get before you could so quickly dismiss your brother's death. I suddenly had a sense of overwhelming gratitude that I hadn't been forced to get to know Jaret any better. If Tavas was that detached from his brother, and the Fae Queen wanted to kill Tavas based on the crimes committed by Jaret, I felt lucky to have had such limited time with him.

"So what does that mean for the Dragon Queen?" I asked.

"It means she'll have to find her own agenda," Tavas said. "She's got a destructive nature, but she's patient and doesn't have any resources yet, so she'll wait. Build up alliances, and find the right time to strike."

"She's a shifter, isn't she?" I already knew the answer, but I had to check.

"Yes," Tavas said. "Which means, she could be anywhere by now."

"You think she would have gone along with Jasmine's plan?" I didn't even know what Jasmine wanted with the dragon queen, but if this queen was so powerful, why would she take orders from a mage?

"Jasmine and the others didn't raise the queen for her cause; they did it for their own." Tavas stopped walking, and readjusted James, then moved forward again.

"What do you mean?" I asked.

"There's supposed to be something mystical or magical that happens to those with dragon ancestry if they help participate in the raising of a queen. I'm guessing Jasmine wanted that power.

Though the queen would have destroyed her soon enough anyway."

"So, they thought they would get power and that maybe they could control her?" I asked.

"Something like that," Tavas said.

I stumbled over loose rock and grabbed Tavas's arm to steady myself. "Sorry."

"Be careful, little dragon," Tavas said. "We can't have you getting yourself killed just yet."

"What's that supposed to mean?" I asked.

"Well, if we want to stop the queen from her evil plans, we're going to need you." Tavas made it sound like it was common knowledge and like he was planning to help.

"You'd help with that?" I asked.

"I was alive the last time this bitch was in power, trust me, we're all screwed if she gains her strength and builds alliances." Tavas turned and cut through a group of trees.

I wasn't even sure where we were or what the plan was. I'd just been blindly following Tavas down the mountainside. "Where are we going?"

"Back to the car," Tavas said.

Just then, I saw the path in front of us. Tavas must have a hell of a sense of direction.

After a few more silent minutes on the trail, I saw street lamps ahead, illuminating the trailhead parking area. My heart leaped as I saw the unmistakable silhouette of people standing around the waiting car.

"Go on," Tavas said.

Breaking into a run, I dashed down the last portion of the trail, careful to pick my feet up to avoid loose rocks.

As I neared the parking lot, I made out the familiar faces of McKenzie, Dima, and Alec. Along with Lyla and the mages we'd rescued.

Laughing, I ran right into the middle of my friends who caught me in a group hug. I turned to Alec. "Where were you?"

"We ran into some troll trouble," he said, as everyone backed up to give me some space. "I was able to avoid capture, and they asked me to find you. I never did, so I came back to the car, hoping you were here already." He frowned. "I seem to miss all the fun."

"I might have to stay with you next time," I said. "I've had enough fun."

Tavas arrived at the car then, James now cradled in his arms like a child. "We need to get him to a healer."

"I can do it," McKenzie said. "Healing is my best skill."

Tavas looked at me skeptically.

After everything McKenzie and I had been through, she had shown that she was tough, and honest, and could use her magic. I looked at McKenzie's determined expression over to Tavas, then nodded. "Let her do it."

Tavas gently set James on the ground, and a small group gathered nearby to watch.

"Morgan!" Lyla walked over to me. Her red hair was a pile of tangled knots, her face was dirty, and she had streaks down her cheeks showing that she'd been crying.

I embraced my friend. "Thank the gods you're safe. Are you hurt?"

She shook her head. "No, they hardly fed us and they kept us locked up, but until this," she showed me the slice on her forearm, the one that matched mine, "they didn't harm us."

The other mages were standing near her as if they weren't sure if I was a good guy or a bad guy. They needed support, they needed someone to see if they were okay, and they needed to get home.

With a last glance at McKenzie leaned over James, I decided

that as much as I wanted to watch her heal him, it would be better if I found a way to help.

"Can you introduce me?" I asked Lyla, lifting my chin toward the four other women.

The women were huddled behind her, looking just as disheveled and tired as Lyla, but they all seemed to be healthy considering everything they'd been through. "Hi, I'm Morgan."

I waved at the mages. "I came here to get you all home, and that's what I'm going to do, okay?"

"Who sent you?" A brunette asked.

"Nobody, really," I said. "I wanted to find my friends."

"You don't work for the Order?" A smaller mage asked. She looked like she was in her early teens.

"No," I said without hesitation. "Never have, never will."

"What happened? Why did they take us?" the teenager asked.

"They didn't tell you anything?" I asked.

All the women shook their heads.

"They said something about the future and a ritual," Lyla said. "Other than that, they were pretty quiet about the details."

Trying to figure out the best way to share everything, I took a deep breath and blew it out slowly. "Well, it turns out we all have something in common. We all have dragon ancestors."

"Are you saying we're Dragon Bloods?" Someone asked.

"We are nothing like those brutes," the teenager said.

"Just because we have dragon blood, doesn't mean we have to be like them," I said. "There's some good to having dragon blood as a mage."

"Like what?" Lyla asked.

"Let's get you all home first, then we can figure it out, okay?" I said.

"How are we getting back?" the teenager asked.

"I called in a favor," Tavas said from behind me.

I turned to look at him, wondering how long he'd been standing behind me. "What kind of favor?"

"Cut me some slack, okay little dragon?" he said, then walked back over to where James was still unmoving on the ground.

"Who's that? He's cute," the teenager said.

"No," I said. "Absolutely not. In fact, why don't you all wait in the car? I'm going to check on the others, and I'll keep you posted."

"Come on, Lucy," Lyla said, leading the teenage girl to the car with the others.

I heard the car doors opening and closing as I walked over to where James was still on the ground. Alec was staring at him with concern written on his face.

A few steps away from James, I hesitated, pausing my progress. What if he didn't wake up? What if this was it?

"He's going to be fine," Tavas said. "It just might take some time for him to recover fully. Being forced in and out of his dragon state takes a lot out of him."

"Thanks," I said, hoping Tavas was right. I continued my progress toward the grounded dragon shifter.

Kneeling down next to McKenzie, I sat while she worked. James's shirt had been cut away, showing he was just as muscular as he seemed in his tight tee-shirts. But right now, I wasn't paying attention to any part of him other than the wound in his side.

McKenzie had managed to slow the bleeding, but the wound didn't seem to want to close. James looked pale and weak. I wondered how much blood he'd lost already.

"Can you give him blood?" Dima asked Alec.

McKenzie looked up from James's wound. "I don't think that's a good idea for a dragon. We don't know what it could do to him."

Then, McKenzie glanced over at me, noticing that I'd joined the group. "You have to try."

"Try what?" I asked.

"Healing. Maybe it would be better coming from another dragon," she said.

"I'm not a healer," I said.

"Like hell, you're not," she said. "You've done more than your share of healing over the last few days."

She was right. I had done a lot more magic than I was used to and all of it had been successful.

"Okay," I said, taking McKenzie's place as she moved aside for me. If there was a chance that I could help him, I was going to try it.

32

*T*ension twisted and turned inside me, winding and unwinding like a spring that was ready to release. How was I supposed to do this?

My hands hovered over James's wound. I knew the spell I should be using, I remembered the words, and despite the magic I'd already used today, I was still buzzing with power. For a moment, I wondered if Tavas's dragon was still around, but knew that could wait. Right now, I had to try the healing spell on James.

With a deep breath, I concentrated on what I needed to do. Nobody else mattered right now. Just me and James.

I mouthed the words to the spell and focused on sending all of the magic I had left into James. He had to wake up. I needed him to wake up. This couldn't be the end for him.

Time seemed to stop as I waited, holding my breath while I watched James's face for any sign of life. Words sounded from behind me, but I couldn't make them out. I was too focused on the injured dragon.

After what felt like an eternity, his eyelids fluttered. I let out the breath I'd been holding along with a little cry of joy. He moved his head, slowly and then winced, eyes still closed. Leaning over him, I cupped his cheek with my hand. "James, can you hear me?"

His eyelids fluttered again. Then slowly, he opened them. Even the injured eye was able to open partially. After a brief look of confusion, his gaze locked on mine and he smiled. "Hi."

"Hi, yourself," I said.

James grunted as he pushed himself to sitting, then he looked down at his side, his fingers tracing over the dried blood. The wound was now gone. My spell had worked.

"How are you feeling?" I asked.

"I'll live." He brushed a loose strand of hair away from my eyes. "You know, I would never have expected any of this the day you came walking into my house."

I laughed. "Me neither."

Another muffled sound came from behind me somewhere, and I turned at the noise. To my surprise, my friends looked out of focus, like I was viewing them through warped plastic. Panic sprang through me, and I jumped to my feet, worried that the Dragon-Bloods or someone else had found us and cast a spell on them.

James grabbed my hand and tugged me back to him. "Slow down, they're fine."

"You can't see that?" I gestured to where the foggy outlines of Dima, McKenzie, and Alec were waiting for me.

"I can, and it's fine," James said. "Come here." He pulled me down. "You managed a privacy spell. They can't see what we're doing in here. It's like a curtain around us."

"But I can see them," I said, catching sight of the mischievous look in his eye. For a guy who had just suffered a deadly injury, he sure had other things on his mind. Though I had to admit, after the kiss we shared, I was ready to try again.

As if he could read my mind, he wrapped his arm around me

and pulled me closer, his lips right near my ear. "They can't see anything but shadows."

My breathing was already shallow as James's lips brushed across my ear, then moved to my cheek, then gently to my mouth.

This kiss was different than the one in the cave. This time, the pressure was gentle, sweet, comfortable. I wanted to melt into him and never leave the privacy I'd created around the two of us.

Slowly, I pulled away, surprised I had the willpower to break the kiss first. "Please tell me you're sticking around this time."

"I'm not going anywhere until you send me away," James said.

"Don't count on that," I said, a smile on my lips. For the first time in a long time, I was feeling pure joy. James seemed to have a way of making me happy even in the worst situations.

"Now, how do I make this thing go away so we can get everyone home?" I asked.

"Same way you made it," he said. "Think about what you want."

I was sensing a pattern with dragon magic and wondered if I'd ever get used to doing magic without saying the spells out loud. Steeling myself for the questions that were going to be waiting on the other side, I imagined the barrier going away, connecting us with the rest of the world once again.

As my friends came back into focus, I pulled James to his feet. Dima let out a squeal of joy and Alec met James with a handshake. McKenzie seemed to relax visibly. Possibly for the first time since I arrived at the Mage Order.

My jaw tensed as I thought about the betrayal, once again, coming from the Order that my mom had held in such high regard. How long was it going to continue to be a place that could ruin so many lives?

I looked over at McKenzie, who was smiling as Alec introduced her to James. She didn't show any signs of hesitation around meeting a dragon shifter. In fact, on this whole trip, she'd been focused on the goal: saving the missing mages. She hadn't been thrilled with the idea of involving a fae, but she went along with it. She could have stood up for Jasmine. She could have defended her. Instead, she protected the kidnapped mages and helped get them to safety. I'd been wrong about her. McKenzie was one of the good ones, and I had a feeling if I asked her to help me again, she'd be in. Right now wasn't the time for more suicide missions, though. Right now, we needed to get back to Realm's Gate.

After we got the mages back to their families, all I wanted to do was to take a shower and curl up in bed. Possibly with James. But only to sleep, for now.

It had been far too long since I was clean and safe and rested. But there was one more thing we had to do before I could do that. The Mage Order had to pay for what they'd done.

"Right on time," Tavas said, pointing to a pair of headlights coming up the road.

"Your favor?" I asked.

"Yep," he said.

Fingers brushed my fingertips, a hand reaching to clasp mine. James's grip was strong and soothing. I squeezed his hand and watched in silence as a VW Bus pulled into the dirt.

Tavas walked toward the waiting vehicle and greeted the driver with a wave. A woman in tight jeans and a flannel shirt stepped out of the car. Her long blonde hair was in a ponytail high on her head.

"Another fae?" I asked James.

He shook his head. "No, that's Veronica. She's a vampire."

"Hey, James!" The leggy vampire called out as she walked over to where we were standing. "Been a long time."

James let go of my hand and met the newcomer in a hug, then led her over to me. "Veronica, this is Morgan."

"Hi, Morgan." Veronica wrapped me up in a hug, and I awkwardly patted her on the back in response.

She stepped back and surveyed the dirt lot. "So, y'all are in need of a driver?"

"We won't fit in one car," I said.

The driver's door of Dima's car opened, and Lyla stepped out. "This our ride?"

After everything we'd been through to save Lyla and the other mages, I was hesitant to hand them over to a stranger.

"You can trust her," Tavas said.

I opened my mouth to object, but Tavas cut me off. "I know, and you're going to have to let me make that up to you later, but right now, these mages need to get home."

"You can come with us if you want, Morgan," Veronica said. "I promise I'll take good care of your friends."

Taking a deep breath, I nodded. "Thank you, but there's one more thing I have to do." I turned to Alec and Dima. "Can you two go with the mages? And, Dima, can I borrow your car?"

"I can go with them," McKenzie offered.

I shook my head. "I need you with me. You and I have some business with the Mage Order."

McKenzie pursed her lips. "That we do."

Alec tossed me the car keys. "Good luck, see you at home."

"Thanks," I said, catching the keys.

"You boys coming?" I asked Tavas and James.

Tavas smiled. "I thought you'd never ask."

James gave me a quick kiss on the cheek, then took the keys from me. "I'm driving. You tell me everything."

The four of us piled into the car, and within a few minutes of the drive, McKenzie was asleep in the back seat. Surprisingly, I was still feeling alert as I gave James a play-by-play of our adventures.

"A massive spider?" James said.

"It was awful," I said. "Hey, have you heard of a place called Nowhere?"

"Sure," James said. "Don't tell me you wound up in that backward town?"

"Oh yes," I said, going on to tell him about Moonbeam.

Once we got to the part of the story where Tavas came in, he joined in the telling.

"By the way, thanks for the whole binding thing," I said. "I really loved having that one in my head."

"Hey, I can't hear a word anymore, it's absolute bliss," Tavas said.

"It was the only way to make sure he helped you," James said. "Plus, I figured if he spent some time in your head, there was no way he wouldn't grow to like you at least a little bit."

Turning in my chair so I could see Tavas, I smiled at him. "Is that what happened? I was wondering why you hadn't flirted with me or said anything inappropriate in a while."

"You can't prove anything," Tavas said. "Just being respectful of my best mate's girl."

The drive passed quickly, and as the sun was beginning its ascent, we were closing in on Realm's Gate. An odd feeling of deja-vu passed over me. How many times was I going to be driving home after fighting for my life with James by my side?

With the dragon queen free from her prison, I had a feeling this might not be the last time I did this.

The ward shimmered in front of us as we approached. It was odd seeing it back up and running. The rest of the world had moved on, unaware of anything we'd been through. They didn't yet know of the destruction and danger that was waiting for us in the coming months as the dragon queen worked to build her followers. But right now, I didn't want to think about that.

Cold sliced through me as we drove through the barrier, officially back in Realm's Gate.

"McKenzie," I said, gently touching her knee.

"Hmm." The mage pulled her legs away from me, going right back to sleep.

"I'll wake her," Tavas said.

"You sure you're ready to confront the Mage Order?" James asked.

"I have to," I said. "I can't let them get away with this."

"Alright," he said. "Just show me the way there. I'm behind you."

"Thanks," I said.

When we pulled up to the iron gate of the Mage Order, I was surprised to see it was already open. James slowed the car. "Turn here?"

"Yes," I said, unsure of why the gates were open. "McKenzie, those gates usually open?"

"No," McKenzie said.

As soon as James turned the car into the long driveway, I knew why they were open. In front of us were several police cars, all parked in front of the mansion that housed the Order. My heart pounded in my ears. Jasmine had said they were keeping dragon mages here. Had more gone missing? Were they hurt? Were the police in on this?

James parked the car. "You sure you want to go in there?"

I already had my seatbelt off. "Why don't you and Tavas wait here. Give McKenzie and me some time."

"You have ten minutes," Tavas said.

"Thanks." I opened the door and stepped outside, then ducked my head back in. "You're not so bad, yourself, Tavas."

Closing the door behind me, I waited for McKenzie to join me.

"You have a plan, right?" McKenzie asked as we made our way to the front door.

"Sure, confront the Order, see how they react, get the remaining dragon mages out of there." I shrugged. It wasn't really a plan, but it was all I had.

Just then, Chief Matthias walked out of the open double doors, two police officers behind her. Each of the officers had a handcuffed mage with them.

"Morgan?" the chief called to me.

I lifted my hand in greeting, a sheepish smile on my face. I like the chief, and while I thought she was probably one of the good ones, I had too much distrust of authority figures even to consider calling her. Instead, I was here to deliver my own justice, without any sort of plan. Seeing her here made me feel slightly foolish. "Hi, chief."

She shook her head but wore a smile on her face. "I should have known you'd be involved somehow." Then she turned to the officers behind her. "Get those two in for questioning."

The police officers led their prisoners to the cars, and the chief walked over to where McKenzie and I were standing. "I'm guessing you figured out that the Mage Order was infiltrated by the Dragon-Bloods?"

"Jasmine's dead," I said.

The chief didn't even flinch. Instead, she narrowed her eyes and nodded. "I had a feeling it went all the way up to her. What happened?"

"We were sent to find the missing mages," I said.

"There were more?" Chief Matthias asked. "We found six underage mages here. Jasmine had convinced them they were going to die if they left the Order. They've since been returned to their families."

I eyed McKenzie.

"I swear, I didn't know she was telling them that," she said.

"Please tell me the rumors aren't true," Chief Matthias said. "That they weren't playing at raising a dead dragon?"

"Short version," I said. "Yes. And the dragon is back."

"Shit." The chief rubbed her eyes. "And here I was hoping things could get back to normal around here."

"It might be a while before that happens," I said, wishing it weren't the case.

"Right." The chief narrowed her eyes at me. "You know, the Order is going to need new leadership. Someone who has a moral compass that isn't quite so easily fooled. We arrested most of the leadership today. Several members were caught tampering with surveillance after Jimmy's murder. And they called the hunters on you."

It felt like someone was squeezing my insides as her words sunk in. Not only was she confirming the role of the Mage Order in this whole mess, but she was also asking me to step up and be a leader. I didn't even want to be a member of the Mage Order.

Grabbing McKenzie by her shoulders, I pushed her forward. "Chief, McKenzie is the woman for the job."

The chief eyed McKenzie, looking her up and down. "Well, I'm not a member of the Order, so I don't have any say. But I'd guess that in the state they're in, if the two of you make the claim that McKenzie is the one for the job, the rest will follow."

"Morgan, everything okay?" James called out from behind me.

I turned to see him standing next to the car. The door still open beside him.

Chief Matthias moved closer to me, leaning in and lowering her voice. "Now, I don't know about you, but if that is what was waiting for me at home, I would get there as fast as I could." She winked at me, and I felt my cheeks flush.

"You girls get some rest," Chief Matthias called as she walked toward the waiting police car. "I'll be in touch soon."

"She's got a point," McKenzie said. "I can take it from here, Morgan."

"You sure?" I asked, hoping she didn't ask me to get involved with her quest for taking over the Mage Order.

"I've got this," she said. "And thank you. For everything."

"Right back at ya," I said. "I guess some of the Mages in the Order aren't so bad, after all."

We said our goodbyes for now, and I headed back to where James was waiting for me in the car. I settled into the passenger seat. To my surprise, Tavas wasn't in the back seat anymore. "Where'd he go?"

"He had some errands to run, said something about giving us alone time," James said, leaning in close to me.

"Well, thank you, Tavas," I said, matching James's movements and meeting him in the middle for a kiss.

AUTHOR NOTES

Thank you for taking the time to read my book! I hoped you enjoyed your time in Realm's Gate. Book 3 is available for pre-order today!

Please consider leaving a review for this book on Amazon.

Want updates, news, and giveaways?
Join My Mailing List

Also by Dyan Chick
Fae Cursed: Legacy of Magic Book 1
Dark Fae: Legacy of Magic Book 2
Heir of Illaria: Book 1 of the Illaria Series
Oracle of Illaria: Book 2 of the Illaria Series
Battle of Illaria: Book 3 of the Illaria Series

www.dyanchick.com
adhchick@gmail.com

Printed in Great Britain
by Amazon